NOVAK'S MISSION

JAMES H LEWIS

For Albina Senko, who lent me part of her amazing life story

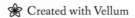 Created with Vellum

AMY O'CONNOR

CHAPTER ONE
AMY'S SECRET

The Boyleston Police Station shouted neglect from its peeling paint to its fusty locker room odor. Karol Novak knew he'd need more than latex and Lysol to rid it of decay. As he readied himself for the challenge, he realized he'd forgotten the access code. Not a promising first act.

He set down the carton cradled in his left arm and rang the buzzer beneath the bulletproof glass panel. A young uniformed woman with a head of tight blonde curls glanced through the window and came around to unlock the door.

"Thanks," he said, "I'm—"

"The new chief. I recognize you. *Entré.*" She performed an awkward curtsy and stood aside as he maneuvered the box through the small entrance area.

"I'm Officer Barnwell," she said, "Lydia."

Novak smiled and nodded as he braced his carton against the door and shoved four others into the bullpen with his foot. "My office is...?"

She led the way, throwing open the door to a windowless room containing a desk, two bookcases, two office chairs in faux leather, a three-drawer filing cabinet, and stained ceiling tiles. "Deputy Chief McMahon has been using this office. He hasn't vacated yet."

Reports and files covered the desk. They transferred Novak's books and mementos from his cartons to the bookcases, refilling the empty ones with McMahon's belongings. Barnwell loaded them onto a dolly and wheeled them down the hall, returning to stand in the doorway as Novak rearranged his collection. "We're glad you're here. Relieved, after all this—" She held up both hands to encompass something she chose not to describe.

"I'm sure you've had a lot of uncertainty." He didn't know what else to say.

"Plenty."

"You're alone on duty?" He tried not to make it sound like a criticism.

"No. We have two patrol cars out, but a delivery truck has just overturned at the entrance to Parkway West. Traffic is backed up all the way to Carnegie. We've rerouted traffic onto Noblestown Road. It's all we can do until Greentree police clear the ramp."

Boyleston was one of 130 municipalities in Allegheny County, ranging in population from Pittsburgh's three hundred thousand to Haysville's seventy. They were served by 109 police agencies, some employing only one officer, many distinguished by their levels of ineptitude. Coordination was spotty. An accident in one could cascade into its neighbors, creating mayhem.

Barnwell watched as Novak unpacked, making him feel as though he were under surveillance. "Who's that?" she said as he hung a framed photo over a protruding nail.

"Petr Čech. He's goalkeeper for Arsenal and for the Czech National team." Seeing her frown of incomprehension, he added, "Soccer."

"What's with the helmet?"

"Several years ago, he saved a goal by covering the ball with his body. An opposing player slid into his head with his cleats raised. He almost died." Novak stared at Čech's image for a moment. "He fought back and is still among the top keepers in the Premier League."

"And that one?"

Novak followed her gaze to a faded photograph of a young man. "Henry Sutton. He was my best friend growing up."

When he didn't elaborate, she said, "Weren't you with the Pittsburgh Bureau?"

"Thirty-three years." Again, he offered nothing more.

Folding her arms, she continued to study him. "Why did you come here, of all places?"

Novak looked up, his perpetual half-smile disappearing. "I live in Boyleston, and they needed me."

"Yes, but what I mean is—"

"I know what you mean," he said. He immediately regretted his sharp tone. "I'm retired, and the council asked me to step in. I feel a duty to help out."

"I'm glad you're here."

"So am I." He smiled and tried to look her in the eye, but found her penetrating gaze intimidating.

She turned, ready to resume her duties, but wheeled again. "Will I be okay?"

He frowned, shaking his head in bewilderment.

"I was one of the officers Chief Russell used on outside assignments. All along, I thought we were working for the borough. Once I realized he was pocketing the money, I reported it to the mayor. I assume he told you."

"No, he hasn't mentioned it. Why would you be in trouble?"

She lowered her voice. "I didn't speak out for a month. I worried he'd retaliate, feared losing my job. When he continued doing it, I worked up the courage."

"This was last fall?"

"No, I spoke out around this time last year. When nothing came of it, I figured no one cared."

Novak looked away to conceal his reaction. She'd reported last spring that Chief Russell was using officers in his private security business, and yet the borough hadn't terminated him until January? As a law officer and taxpayer, Novak was outraged that Russell had been allowed to continue ripping the borough off for eight months or longer.

"I'd appreciate it if you didn't tell the others I was the source," she said. "No one knows where it came from."

"Of course I won't." She exhaled and relaxed her shoulders. "And I don't see how anyone could take issue with it. You did the right thing."

Her face erupted into a smile that crinkled her cheeks, making her eyes even more pronounced. "We have a lot facing us," she said. "What's your top priority?"

He looked down as he considered a response. "Getting the department on track. Keeping everyone alive. These are dangerous times. I want to keep everyone safe."

"And pursuing justice," she said. "We have to pursue justice, don't we?"

He chose not to argue the point.

Barbara Novak arrived home to find her husband kneeling in the bathroom, drawing a bead of caulk around the lip of the bathroom tub. Their home had just passed the century mark, and while it had good bones, Karol spent a few hours each week patching tears in its ligaments, tendons, and muscles.

She sat on the closed toilet lid and waited, a sign that she had something to discuss.

"Nice legs, lady."

She laughed, leaned forward, and planted a kiss on his forehead. "Trying to make an old girl feel good?"

"No, I mean it. You've still got it." Novak had always admired his wife's legs. Barbara Fournier, a second-generation French-Canadian, had been a dancer during her college days. The first time he had spotted her on a warm September day in Schenley Park forty years before, she had been sprawled on a blanket reading a book, her modest shorts displaying the most beautiful set of "stems" he'd ever seen. Karol Novak had come to a full stop during his afternoon run and gawked.

"Hello to you, too," she'd said.

"I'm sorry," he'd stammered, uncertain whether she was pleased or annoyed at his open admiration. "I don't mean to stare." Still fumbling, he'd choked out an introduction.

Accepting his apology, Barbara had patted the blanket alongside her, inviting him to sit and chat. From that moment on, there had been no one else for either of them.

They chased each other for three years while remaining chaste— they were good Catholic kids, after all. She sat in the front row of the stands, watching him tend goal for Pitt's soccer team. He sat alongside her in the cheap seats at Heinz Hall, listening as André Previn led the Pittsburgh Symphony. After graduation, they married at St. Cecilia's, her family's parish church, settling into the three-story brick house, which, like Boyleston Borough itself, had seen better days. Over time, they restored it to its former prominence and built a family.

"How's the police station?" she said, interrupting his reverie.

"Rundown. Depressing." Boyleston's Police Department occupied one-third of the borough office building, which also housed its library. It had been built during the late 1940s when Pittsburgh supplied the nation with all the steel it needed to feed its building boom. While Karol and Barbara had attended council meetings and spent many days at the library, neither had yet ventured into the public safety wing.

"It needs a coat of paint and new radios," he said as he squared off the bead at the corner of the wall. "I don't get it. The federal government has generous equipment grants, but none of it has landed in Boyleston. Someone hasn't been paying attention."

"Too busy running a side business," Barbara said, "and fencing stolen items."

"I met a young officer, a woman, who claims to have reported Russell's scheme more than a year ago."

"But they didn't fire him until the first of the year."

"Eight long months. It does not give me confidence in their judgement."

"But they hired you." He smiled, grateful as always for her unwavering encouragement. "This woman, is she pretty?" The two shared a laugh as Barbara posed the question her mother-in-law liked to ask whenever a young woman came up in conversation.

"No, I wouldn't say that. She's...*interesting*. She has frizzy blonde hair, a nose that's a bit big for her face, and piercing blue eyes that bore into you. She's one hell of an interrogator. She doesn't let up until you answer her question."

"I may have to keep an eye on the two of you."

Karol chuckled. It was part of their game.

"Can you listen to something for a moment?" she said.

At last, he thought, she was ready to impart whatever was on her mind. "I'm married. Listening is what I do."

"What do you know about a man named Thomas Walsh?"

Karol's hand paused. "Just a minute while I finish." Only after he had removed caulk from the gun, cleaned the tools, and placed them in his leather kit did he turn to face her, still crouching, his back to the wall. "Why do you ask about Walsh?"

"I sit here for ten minutes to hear you answer my question with a question."

"It's why I married you. You were the only woman with enough patience."

"Something odd happened at the party." Barbara had spent the day helping their daughter, Mariel, throw a party of some sort. "You know Bridey O'Connor."

"I don't think so."

"Sure you do. She's the single mom who lives a block down from Mariel. Her daughter, Amy, is Jennifer's best friend."

"Uh-huh." It would do no good to dispute the issue. Jennifer, their granddaughter, had dozens of friends, all of whom had at least one parent. Barbara somehow kept track of them all.

"Anyway, it's Amy's birthday, and Mariel threw a party for her at the bowling alley."

"That's generous."

"Bridey doesn't have much money, and since Jennifer and Amy are so close..."

Novak nodded as though he understood.

"They bowled for an hour—Jen had the high score—and then we moved into the restaurant next door for pizza and sodas. Amy opened her presents—what is it about little girls and unicorns?"

"It's the horn."

She ignored him. "We brought out the birthday cake. Bridey lit the candles, told her to make a wish. And Amy sat there thinking about it, looking straight at me."

"At you?"

"Yes. Just hold on a minute. After she blew out the candles, one girl asked what she'd wished for. Another said that she shouldn't tell, or else it wouldn't come true. Amy replied, 'I have to tell. I need Mrs. Novak to hear.'"

Novak, who had only been half listening, now leaned toward her.

"She said, 'I wish Chief Novak can get my pap out of prison.' That was it. The whole place went quiet. No one knew what to say. Bridey gasped, grabbed the girl's arm, and headed toward the exit, leaving her presents behind. The poor child was wailing. I ran after them. I feared what Bridey would do to her."

Novak stroked his cheek as he considered her story. "And her grandfather is Tom Walsh?"

"Yes, but I had to drag it out of her mother as *she* dragged Amy to her car. I felt sorry for her."

"The mother or the daughter?"

Barbara tilted her head from one side to the other. "Both."

"C'mon, let's get out of this ridiculous position and find something to drink."

Staggering to his feet and steadying himself against the wall for a moment, Novak descended the stairway. His hand brushed against a portrait of his paternal grandfather, one of a dozen framed photos of three generations of family members that lined the staircase. After straightening it, he took another flight to the basement, fished a bottle of Yuengling and a can of soda water from the garage refrigerator, and joined his wife in the living room.

————

THEY SAT opposite each other on a long brown sofa that backed to a picture window. Barbara sprawled lengthwise, her feet in his lap as she sipped the beer while Karol faced the gas fireplace, above which hung a Patriarchal cross with its double crossbars.

"Thomas Walsh..." he began.

"Barbara!" came a frail voice from a nearby room.

"I'll go," Novak said.

"Sit still. I'll get her."

With his wife gone to help his mother up after her nap, Novak flipped open his laptop and searched for the name, hoping to recharge his memory of the three-decade-old homicide. He hadn't played any role in the case, but since the murder had taken place less than a half-mile from their home, he had followed it from arrest and conviction to sentencing. A decade-old article from the *Pittsburgh Post-Gazette*, when last Walsh had appealed for clemency, helped fill in the details.

"Hi, Ma, how was the nap?"

His mother muttered an acknowledgment as Barbara eased her into the reclining chair opposite the fireplace. Novak turned on the gas log. Even in summer, any room Izabela Novak entered was too cold for her. He fetched her a glass of wine and placed a blanket over her lap.

"*Na zdravie*," his mother said, raising her glass.

"And cheers to you, Mom." He hoisted the can of soda water.

Barbara was not to be deterred. "Thomas Walsh," she said.

"Walsh, yes. Over the Memorial Day weekend in '89, he went fishing upstate with friends. His wife, Rebecca, was alone with their four-year-old daughter. Someone entered their home and suffocated the mother while she slept. The little girl discovered her body in the morning and ran across the street to neighbors. At first, county detectives suspected an intruder, but Walsh's alibi didn't hold up, and they recovered evidence from his car. They charged him with her murder."

"Bridey was the little girl?"

"A terrible thing. No child should have to face that. Anyway, Walsh denied it at first but then confessed. He was sentenced to life without parole but immediately recanted and started filing appeals. They all failed. A decade ago, he appealed for clemency, but the governor turned him down."

"Do you think he's guilty?"

Novak shrugged. "He confessed. A jury convicted him. Why should I doubt it?"

"He was a bad man," his mother said. She'd been following the conversation, offering no opinion until now.

"Still, will you look into it?" Barbara said.

"I can't." When she turned a rare frown his way, he said, "Although it took place in Boyleston, the county handled it, as they do every crime of violence. I haven't yet assumed command, but I'm sure the department has a full plate. Plus, we have nothing to go on— no new information, no sign that there was anything wrong with the conviction."

"All you have is a nine-year-old girl's birthday wish."

"Nice try."

Barbara smiled as though giving up, though Novak doubted he'd heard the end of it.

———

"Won't you come in with me?" Izabela remained in the passenger seat as the car idled, willing her son to join her at early Mass.

"I can't, Mom." Novak stared straight ahead, unwilling to meet his mother's gaze.

She did not move. "Why don't I walk you in?" he said, attempting to break the spell.

"No. I can take care of myself." She opened the passenger door, then leaned over to peer back in. "You can't hold this anger inside you. It's not right, not healthy."

"It's perfectly healthy," he said, still refusing to meet her eye.

"Your father—"

"—would have felt the same." Which was untrue.

"You should return," she said in a softer tone. When he didn't answer, she said, "I'm worried about you, Karol."

"I assure you, my soul is in good hands."

"No, I'm worried about *you*. You look tired. You're under too much stress."

"I'm fine, *Mamička*," he said, hoping the childhood endearment would placate her.

"Are you sure you should take this on? You don't need to."

"I'm fine," he repeated, and immediately regretted his sharp tone.

She sighed and, gathering up all the strength in her 84-year-old body, slammed the door before stalking toward the entrance. Despite the line of cars gathered behind him in the circular driveway, Novak waited until the heavy wooden doors of the ancient church had closed behind her before driving away.

St. Cyril and Methodius Church, one of Pittsburgh's Slovakian parishes, had been her home and refuge since her arrival in the United States at the end of the war. Here, Slovak-speaking nuns had taught her to read, write, and speak English. Here, her younger brother and sister, both born in the US, had been baptized. Here, both she and her sister had married beneath its arched wooden timbers.

The diocese was studying parish consolidation, and Karol Novak suspected that St. Cyril would not survive the process. Not wanting to alarm her, he had not told his mother that she might soon lose her church home.

It was one of several things he kept from her, some of which were known only to police officers. And to the church.

CHAPTER TWO
THE HOLDUP

Mayor Fred Tifton had asked Novak to come first to his office before reporting for duty, but when Novak arrived Monday morning, the mayor's assistant reported he was already in the police wing. Novak checked his watch. He was ten minutes early. The assistant led him down a hallway and punched in the code to unlock the door to the department.

"Ah, there he is," Tifton said as Novak entered the bullpen. The mayor stood surrounded by eight uniformed officers, three plain-clothes investigators, a dispatcher, and an administrative assistant, some perched on chairs or desks around the room, others leaning against the walls.

"Am I late?"

"No. Everyone else was here, so I figured we'd get started," Tifton said without further explanation. The mayor, who'd held office for over a decade, was in his seventies, with receding sandy hair and deep bags under his gray, clouded eyes. His dour expression and marionette mouth suggested a man who'd seen it all and disapproved of most of it.

Turning to the officers, he said, "Let me introduce Karol Novak. He's local. Lived in Boyleston all his life. I'm sure many of you have run into him. We pulled him out of retirement to serve as chief, at least until he returns the department to a stable footing. I don't know how long that'll take, but the council and I will monitor progress."

Novak opened his mouth to respond, but Tifton forged ahead. "I won't tell you what a setback this has been for the community." Then he did just that. "We've worked hard to bring new business to Boyleston—create jobs and attract new residents so we get our fair share of Pittsburgh's revitalization. But this..."

Tifton shook his head, his wattle trailing behind. One of the investigators covered his mouth and feigned a cough as he suppressed laughter. The mayor appeared not to notice. "We hired Novak to restore the good name of this department and the borough. I expect you to cooperate with him." He fixed his mirthless eyes on each of them, then turned to Novak. "Do you have anything to add?"

"No, Mr. Mayor. Thank you." As Tifton turned to leave, Novak silently motioned the officers to remain in place. Novak stepped forward and put his hand on a desk to steady himself. When the connecting door closed, he said, "That was uplifting." A few chuckled, but most showed no emotion, not reacting to his sarcasm.

"As the mayor says, I'm a native. I attended St. Cyril's through grade school, finished at Boyleston High, then on to Pitt. I spent thirty-three years with the Pittsburgh Police Bureau—the last eight as chief of detectives. Please introduce yourselves and give me a brief bio."

At first, they looked at one another as though waiting to see who would start. "I only attended public schools," one investigator said. "The nuns wouldn't have me."

His fellow officers laughed, then the rest opened up, punctuating their life stories with other bits of good-natured humor. As each spoke, Novak jotted in a stenographer's notebook, occasioning a few side glances among the officers.

When the last officer had finished, Novak said, "I serve at the pleasure of the council, just as Mayor Tifton does." He saw no need to remind them that, in the scandal's wake, the council had removed

Tifton from the chain of command. No matter how uncomfortable Novak was at the prospect of answering to seven bosses, it beat reporting to the mayor.

"I'll serve as long as they are satisfied with the job I'm doing," he said. Several officers exchanged glances, a few smiled, and one let out a satisfied sigh. "I intend to focus on the present and work toward the future—not get mired in what's gone on before."

Norma Showalter, the administrative assistant, tried to initiate a round of applause but stopped, embarrassed, when no one joined in. A few rewarded Novak with smiles, however, and he could sense most of the men and women had relaxed.

"Questions?" he said.

Lydia Barnwell raised her hand. "You're in this long-term? The mayor made it sound like you're only a caretaker."

"I'm here as long as I can be useful," he said, "and as long as the council wants me."

DEPUTY CHIEF DARYL MCMAHON wore a half-smile as he loped into Novak's office without knocking. He draped his long frame over one of the two office chairs, sitting crosswise with one leg resting on the right arm. Novak placed him at about six-four, slender despite his height, his face and body all angles and crags. A long, thin nose was perched above a compressed mouth, his blond hair clipped in a short, military-style cut.

"I suppose you want to know what we've got going," McMahon said. Novak had asked him in after the meeting, and he seemed to take it as a summons. The deputy had applied for the chief's job; Novak wondered whether he harbored resentment.

"Let's first get better acquainted," he said. "Tell me a bit more about yourself."

McMahon shrugged. "Not much to tell. Like I said, I've been

with the force for two years. Chief Russell brought me on from a small police force in Ohio, where I was chief."

"Where was that?"

"A small town between Toledo and Cleveland."

"Where? Norwalk? Sandusky?"

"Doubleday," he said. "One of those places where they print 'Welcome' on both sides of the same sign."

"And before that?"

"I was with a campus police force for several years."

"Which one?"

"Norwalk State."

Novak wrote a few lines in his notebook. "Is something wrong?" McMahon said.

"Not at all." In an effort to put him at ease, he detailed his own career, but the deputy seemed to pay little attention. Novak figured everyone on the force had been vetting him from the moment word got out that he would be leading the department, so he switched gears. "What are our most pressing current cases?" he said.

"A guy held up a convenience store Saturday night. Asian, I think, though it's hard to tell since he was wearing a nylon stocking over his head. Not Black, anyway. He made off with about $375. Didn't pull a weapon, so we haven't turned it over to the county."

Most municipalities in Allegheny County lacked a crime lab, so they turned to the County PD whenever they needed help with forensic examinations, including all homicides and crimes of violence. McMahon should have done so in this instance, but Novak kept the thought to himself. This was only his first day, and he needed to assess current practices before making changes. He posed a few questions to make certain they had followed procedure—viewing surveillance videos, dusting for prints, patrolling the area for signs of the robber.

Satisfied with McMahon's responses, he said, "Anything else?"

"We broke up a couple of domestics over the weekend. One guy over on Farmington beat up his wife pretty good, but she won't press charges." Something about the way he said it put Novak on edge, but again he withheld criticism.

"Our biggest headache is a bunch of A-holes breaking the speed limit on Corcoran outside Boyleston Elementary," McMahon said. "They ignore the blinking yellows and go barreling through at thirty, thirty-five miles an hour."

"How are we handling it?"

"Don't worry. We've got it covered."

"*How* are we covering it?"

"We send a patrol car once a week and park it at the south end with lights flashing. That slows 'em down."

"But the remaining four days..."

"We don't have that many units, and since the state won't allow us to use radar..." He finished the unspoken thought with a sneer.

Novak could remain passive no longer. "Let's position a VASCAR unit every day this week, then taper off next week to every other day."

"That's a lot of manpower," McMahon said.

His patience at an end, Novak said, "We'd use more if some kid got hurt...or worse. See to it. What else?"

"Aren't you going to ask what I knew about Chief Russell's side business?"

"I'm sure the Allegheny PD turned over everything relevant to the mayor and town council. Unless there's something you want to tell me."

McMahon shifted in his chair. "May I speak frankly?"

"Always."

He looked around him as though someone might be listening. "Officer Barnwell—the girl—she got this whole thing started. She reported him."

"Are you certain about this?"

McMahon snorted, as though the question were unworthy of being asked.

"How did you learn this?"

"Sources," McMahon said, then pinched his lips between thumb and forefinger.

Novak leaned forward, planted his elbows on the desk, and rested his chin on his knuckles. "Who else knows this?"

Again, McMahon didn't provide a direct answer, spreading his arms out to encompass everyone.

"How do they feel towards her?"

McMahon looked Novak in the eye, like a father addressing an errant child. "It's a dangerous business. We can't operate as a team if we can't trust one another."

"He stole from the borough," Novak said, "time, resources, equipment."

McMahon cocked his head, his surprise evident. "I'm not defending him. I'm the one who had to pick up the slack. I'm just saying officers don't rat on each other."

"He undermined public confidence in this department, making the job of every officer more difficult. Someone had to stop it." Novak waited for a reaction but got only a bland stare. "I would have great difficulty with anyone who exacted retribution on an officer who tries to do what's right. Is that clear?"

McMahon nodded.

"That is all. Please close the door when you leave."

Novak began to write, his eyes veering off the page, his head turning to the right. He moaned, placed both hands flat on his desk, and fixed his gaze on the office door until the moment passed, wondering all the while who had "ratted" on Lydia Barnwell.

OVER THE PAST FEW DAYS, Novak had studied the policy manual and recruitment procedures, both of which were inadequate and would require his attention. Now he prowled the office space, exploring the layout, viewing the large, glossy borough map through new eyes, and peering into the few offices surrounding the bullpen.

"What's in this room?" he said as he halted before a locked wooden door with chipped white veneer.

Norma Showalter rushed to his side. "That's our supply room. It's, uh...we have a little problem."

As she unlocked the door, Novak made ready to step inside, then stopped. "What is this?" Fluffy white rolls wrapped in plastic jammed the small room from floor to ceiling.

"It's toilet paper."

"I see that, but what—?"

A small crowd of officers gathered around them.

"It appeared in December," she said.

"Appeared? You just opened the door one morning, and there it was?"

"Something like that."

Novak thought for a moment. "I take it my predecessor had money left in the budget at year-end and thought he'd keep the department well stocked."

Norma nodded while two officers snickered.

"What should we do with it?" she said. "Whenever we need to get a piece of equipment out, we have to move all this crap into the bullpen, then move it all back in again."

"I suppose we should be diligent about using it," Novak said to loud guffaws. As the group broke up, he asked her for a copy of the previous year's budget report. In his office, he confirmed his suspicion. Chief Jason Russell, sensing that the county's probe was closing in, had spent the last six weeks of the previous year in a spending frenzy that rivaled a Black Friday sale at Walmart.

Besides toilet paper, Russell had purchased four sets of walkie-talkies that were on civilian frequencies, two dozen neon green safety vests, six electronic tablets, twenty-four boxes of ammunition that fit no weapons the department used, and a security camera system that was redundant considering the more advanced system that already covered every square foot of the department's interior and exterior. Having read the county's investigative report, Novak knew that

Russell had sold all except the safety vests and ammunition—and apparently the toilet paper—through online auctions. The ammunition had ended up in the retail stock of a local gun store. The man had been rapacious.

Novak spent the afternoon drafting a lengthy memo to the borough's auditor requesting that she declare the toilet paper surplus so the borough could distribute it to other departments, schools, and nonprofit organizations.

Russell had cost Novak most of his first day. He wondered what other potholes lay ahead.

NOVAK LAY STILL for several minutes after he awakened. He twisted onto his left side, trying not to disturb Barbara, and focused on his late father's portrait on the bedroom wall. He remained in that position for a minute. Lowering his feet to the floor, he lifted himself into a sitting position, still staring at the photograph. He rose, took a deep breath, and ventured a few tentative steps toward the bedroom door.

"How is it?"

"I'm sorry. I didn't mean to wake you," he said, avoiding her question.

"What time is it?"

"Nearly six."

"Time to get up, anyway."

"It will reach eighty-five today."

"That's nuts," she said.

"You've been waiting for summer."

"Yeah, but a forty-degree swing in four days...are they trying to kill us?"

Suppressing a grin, he shuffled to the kitchen, ground four measures of coffee, put water on to boil, and poured raisin bran into two bowls, slicing a banana over the cereal. His wife padded in as he poured the water over the coffee grounds and depressed the filter.

"Busy day?" he asked. His mother slept late on all mornings but Sunday, so breakfast was a rare moment of privacy in their daily schedules.

"The superintendent is making his semi-annual pilgrimage. I'm looking forward to it. It's our chance to shine." Barbara was the principal of Washington Middle School, one of three in a district that served four boroughs.

"You always do." He shared with her his visits to business owners, clergy, and other civic leaders over the past week. He'd even introduced himself to the other public and parochial school principals, even though he already knew most of them through Barbara.

"Did you visit Father Murray?" Since most Boyleston residents were Catholic, Father Thomas Murray of St. Cyril and Methodius Church would have topped the list of local clerics. Novak didn't answer as he poured her a cup of coffee.

"I ran into Marilyn Bonner yesterday," she said, breaking the uncomfortable silence. "She said to thank you again for the—what do you call it?"

"Targeted enforcement."

"She's noticed how traffic has slowed outside the school. She's been complaining about it for months, but no one addressed it until you took over. You're her hero."

Novak sighed. "So she told me Tuesday. Such a simple thing. What have they been doing all this time?"

They ate in silence for a few minutes, then Barbara opened a sheet of paper that was folded in a bowl in the middle of the table. "Deputy," she said.

"Daryl McMahon."

"Detectives."

"Mark Ewer, Gordon Horvath, and..."

She waited until he signaled to her by spinning his right index finger in the air. "Black," she said. "Your Black officer. He often plays infield."

"Calvin Mayfield. Jesus!"

"Uniforms."

Novak recited a list of names, missing a veteran officer and one other. "Your great-aunt's name and water on the farm," she prompted.

"Lydia Barn-well," he said, enunciating it. "How could I forget her?"

"How indeed?" she said with an impish grin. "You did well. Better than yesterday."

"I should know them all by now. It's discouraging. I hope I've done the right thing."

She laid her hand over his. "You have," she said. "Remember, Marilyn has been trying to slow traffic for nearly a year. You did it."

"Tah-dah!" Novak said, but he didn't accompany it with a smile.

———

AJAI PATEL SAT on the stool behind the counter of his convenience store, peering at Novak through overlarge glasses. His dark hair cascaded over his eyes; his hand, as he raised his arm to shove it back into place, shook.

"Tell me anything you remember about the man," Novak said. Patrol Officer David Kimrey, taking him at his word to alert the chief whenever the need arose, had summoned him to this convenience store holdup at half past eleven. Despite the hour, Novak was alert and eager to participate.

Patel gave a detailed description of the assailant. "He wore a black and yellow jacket that was too big for him. It hung almost to his knees."

"Which team, do you know?"

"Pirates, Steelers, Penguins—they all have the same colors."

Novak urged him to continue. "He had a baseball cap with some sort of writing on it pulled low on his head and a stocking over his face, so his features were..."

"Distorted," Novak suggested as Patel searched for the right word. "Was he White, Black, Hispanic, Asian...?"

"He had an accent, I think. Skin a bit lighter than mine. Black hair. He held his hand in his left pocket as though he had something in it." Patel pulled his left hand to one side to indicate the weapon the suspect may or may not have been clutching.

Novak complimented him on his detailed description. Patel allowed himself a small smile of triumph and described how he'd estimated the man's height by comparing him to the display rack behind where he'd stood.

"He may be a half-inch above or below five-ten, but no more," Patel said, "and he's left-handed. That was the hand he held in his pocket, but he withdrew it when he went for my money. He wore plastic gloves, the kind food service workers use, and blue athletic shoes."

"Did he have an actual weapon?"

"I didn't ask."

Novak nodded and asked him to describe the conversation.

"He ordered me to hand over the money."

"Do you recall his exact words?"

"'Empty your till and you won't get hurt.' He may be the fellow who held up my cousin's store last week. I told him we're poor people. He said, 'Stop talking.'"

"You and your cousin both own convenience stores?"

"And my brother, Aditya. Everyone calls him Adi."

Novak nodded. He knew Adi and liked him.

Patel described withdrawing ones, fives, tens, and twenties from the drawer. "He told me to pull out the till and give him the big bills. I explained I accept nothing larger, but I had a few more twenties, so I gave them to him. He wanted the cash bag beneath the counter. I told him it was empty, that most people use credit cards." Patel placed an empty canvas pouch on the counter to illustrate the point.

Another cruiser pulled into the lot. Officer Barnwell emerged, joining the others in the convenience store. Novak relayed Patel's description of the holdup man. "He's five-ten, left-handed, possibly foreign, brown skin, brown eyes, straight black hair, wearing faded jeans, an oversized black and gold jacket from one of the local teams —he doesn't recall which one—and blue sneakers."

"Bright blue," Patel added. "I've never seen a pair like them."

"He left on foot," Novak told Kimrey and Barnwell. "I doubt he's still in the neighborhood, but search anyway."

The two officers joined each other in one patrol car and roared out of the parking lot, cruising down Mason Avenue in what would prove to be a fruitless search.

Minutes after they left, a detective from the Allegheny Police Department arrived, followed by a unit from the crime lab. Novak handed the case over, briefing them on everything Patel had told him even though he knew the detective would ask the man to repeat his story.

"If it's the same guy, it's the second convenience store he's struck in a week," Novak said. "Our people failed to notify you of a previous one."

"They should have."

"It won't happen again," he said. "Two holdups in the same neighborhood within days. He's either desperate or foolhardy. We need to stop him before he hurts someone. Or worse."

CHAPTER THREE
AN ENEMY AND A VICTIM

Novak arrived Thursday morning to find his deputy chief meeting with Byron Frain, one of the seven borough council members. He poked his head into McMahon's office and said hello. They returned his greeting but revealed nothing about the subject of their conversation. Novak raised an inquiring eyebrow at his deputy.

"Yesterday morning, an officer stopped *Councilman* Frain," McMahon said, emphasizing the title, "in the speed trap outside the school. I'm taking it off the record."

"You'll do no such thing," Novak said. "This isn't a speed trap. We're enforcing the law to protect the safety of our youngsters. We administer it impartially. Sorry, Councilman."

"The department has shown us courtesy in the past," Frain said, rising from his chair to be eye level with the chief. "We spend hours working for the borough for no pay."

"I respect what you do," Novak said, "and I respect you. But you've hired me to restore confidence in this agency. That means treating every citizen the same—no special favors. I regret any misunderstanding."

Frain moved past him, paused in the narrow hallway, and said, "I voted for you over the objections of the mayor and Councilman Jackson." He stalked out.

"That wasn't smart," McMahon said. "He's a great friend to the department, but he can be a dangerous foe."

"We're not here to make friends," Novak said. "Our job is to enforce the laws. Let him plead not guilty before the magisterial judge and take his chances; we can't play favorites."

"Like assigning extra shifts because your wife's a principal?"

Novak ignored the barb. "If we have other such arrangements, tell me about them. And all future communications with the borough council, the mayor, or any other officials go through me. Is that clear?"

McMahon scratched his chest with his fingernails, not making eye contact.

"Do you understand, Deputy?"

McMahon gave a slight nod and rose to leave.

"One more thing. On Monday, you told me about the convenience store robbery over on Douglas. There was another last night. Same MO, same description of the perp. We called the county in. We should have done that last week."

McMahon shrugged. "We handled it ourselves."

That attitude again. *We can handle it.*

"Our policy is to refer any crime of violence to the county—"

"There was none here."

"He may have had a gun. He didn't show it, but his body language suggested he was armed, correct?"

No answer.

"This guy has struck twice at shops blocks apart. That's reckless, and reckless people worry me. We're a small department. I'll take any help we can get."

NOVAK HAD SCHEDULED meetings with the detective sergeants that morning. He began with Gordon Horvath, the most senior of the three.

Horvath was a formidable presence, standing at six-foot-one with the beefy physique of a linebacker, which he had been at Penn State. His black hair was slicked back from all sides and met in a confluence of inky rivulets at his neckline. His swarthy face seemed chiseled from granite; a scar extended from his left cheekbone to his jawline. He lowered himself into the chair in front of Novak's desk as though it might crumple under his weight.

"We worked together..." Novak said.

"On the Pennfield Avenue jewelry heist," Horvath finished. "Our team began the investigation as a local incident. You connected it to another in Pittsburgh and a third in Aspinwall. We did a composite of all the witness statements and surveillance videos, and you zeroed in on a couple brothers from East Pittsburgh."

"We made joint arrests and made them stick." Novak smiled at the memory. "Now, we work together."

"Yeah."

Novak couldn't tell whether Horvath was unenthusiastic or simply acknowledging reality. "What are your major cases?"

The convenience store robberies headed Horvath's list. There was also a series of vehicle break-ins, a driver who'd fled the scene after striking a pedestrian on Lowell, and a drive-by shooting down in The Shanties. Allegheny County PD was in charge of that one. "But I'm working with them. They like local eyes and ears. If that's okay with you."

"Of course," Novak said, wondering why he felt the need to ask. "These robberies worry me. He's careless, hitting two stores in the same neighborhood only days apart. He's not smart. Nothing's more dangerous than a stupid man with a gun."

"He may be an addict," Horvath offered.

"Which means he's desperate, which makes him even more dangerous. If you see this as your case—" Horvath nodded that he did. "—drop everything else and focus on it. Detective Carpenter is working this for Allegheny."

"I know him. Good man."

"Call him and offer your services." Novak scribbled notes to himself while Horvath waited. "What's your sense of how things are running here?" he asked when he'd finished.

The detective shrugged. "Okay. We're getting our work done. Chief Russell left five months ago and didn't do much while he was here. We've learned to run the place ourselves."

"Are there any procedural changes you'd like to see?"

"That's up to you. I don't concern myself with policy. There's a book, and I go by it."

Horvath appeared to be waiting for the next question. Novak puzzled over how to draw him out.

"I'll tell you one thing," Horvath said with sudden energy. "We need better gear. Half the local agencies use body cameras; we don't. We lack even dashcams, and two of our patrol vehicles are falling apart." He launched into a shopping list of other equipment and repair needs while Novak took notes. There was nothing on Horvath's list he hadn't already noticed, but he wanted to seem receptive.

Novak thanked him and then said, "One more thing. Do you recall the Rebecca Walsh murder case?"

The detective scowled and wrinkled his nose as though he'd detected a foul odor. "That was way back. I've been here for fifteen years. It was long before that."

"Has anyone ever raised questions about it?"

"No. Why would they? Has something changed?"

"A citizen mentioned it. It made me curious." He shrugged to suggest it was unimportant.

"County would have handled it."

Novak agreed, thanked him, and rose, ending the interview. Sergeant Mark Ewer stood outside the office when Horvath emerged. The detective raised his shoulders as he passed, as if to suggest he wasn't sure what *that* was about. Novak pretended not to notice as he welcomed the second detective to sit down.

If Horvath was intimidating, Ewer was disarming. His ready smile in a cherubic face made him seem an innocent choir boy. And whereas Horvath was reticent, Ewer was garrulous. To every question, he responded with a torrent of words, as though a lifetime of thoughts had been dammed up within him and Novak had opened the sluice. He described every case he was working on in minute detail—witness statements, evidence, current status, and next steps. After every response, he would move on to the next before Novak had finished writing.

When Novak probed about conditions within the department, Ewer replied that everything was great and ran down a list of what he found unique about every officer. What was missing? "Teamwork," Ewer said. "Team building. We should get together more often as a group. I'm reading a book written by a management consultant..."

He droned on for more than a minute while Novak wondered how to stop him. "Aren't you taking notes?"

Shaking himself awake, Novak said, "No need to. I've read the same book." He regretted the lie, but it was necessary if he was to keep Ewer from running through lunch and into the dinner hour. "Have you heard of the Becky Walsh case?"

Ewer didn't hesitate. "Sure. Her husband killed her. He returned from a fishing trip to find her in bed with another man. He beat her to death while the other guy fled." Ewer continued his narrative, little of which matched what Novak had already learned from news reports.

Novak thanked and dismissed him, as Ewer seemed ready to launch into an exposition of another old but unrelated case.

"Do you need a break?" Sergeant Calvin Mayfield said on entering, without a trace of irony. Was he acknowledging that an hour of listening to Ewer was a draining experience? But as the young sergeant began answering his questions, Novak suspected Mayfield was more concerned with the chief's ability to absorb important information. When asked, he dwelled not just on active cases, but also on those the department had opened weeks and months before without resolving. As Novak began his furious note-taking, Mayfield said, "I can send you a summary if it would help."

"Please do," Novak said. He put down his pen and gave the young sergeant his full attention. Mayfield was in his mid-thirties, of medium height, with dusky brown skin, close-cropped black hair, and a broad nose that quivered as he spoke. His speech was slow and deliberate, as though he weighed every word before speaking, but it was not halting; his brain seemed to compose the next sentence as he spoke the present one.

When asked about the current state of departmental affairs, Mayfield took in his breath and said, "May I speak frankly, sir?"

The second time someone had posed that question this morning. "That's what I expect from my officers."

"We're a dysfunctional organization. We've had no leadership for two years, perhaps longer. Everyone is in his own orbit, with no sun at the center." He described multiple incidents of officers tripping over each other or missing important aspects of investigations, referring to "officer 1" and "officer 2" without naming names.

"We do not coordinate with other agencies. Many crimes extend beyond our three square miles. We operate only in this borough, but criminals are oblivious to jurisdictional lines." He described a series of missed opportunities and botched investigations, once again using placeholders rather than naming the officers involved.

"How did things get to this point?" Novak asked.

"Chief Russell was distracted, sir, and left everything to the deputy."

"And the deputy chief...?"

"McMahon was trying to do both his own job and the chief's. It was a heavy load."

Novak nodded, appreciative of Mayfield's insistence on addressing problems rather than personalities. As Novak rose to thank him, Mayfield said, "You asked Sergeant Horvath about the Walsh murder."

"Yes. Are you familiar with it?"

"No, sir, but I've asked Ms. Showalter to retrieve our files from storage. I hope that's all right."

"Excellent, Sergeant," he said, pleased at the man's initiative.

"I doubt you'll find much. We would have handed it off to Allegheny County PD."

"I'm sure you're correct."

"May I ask, Chief, why we're interested in it?"

We, not you. "I don't know that we are, but a citizen has asked me to review the case. I want to assure myself that this department conducted itself professionally. We are not reopening it."

"THAT'S INSOLENT," Barbara said the following morning as Novak told her about his conversation with McMahon, "implying you're enforcing the speed limit just to placate me. How did you respond?"

"I wasn't about to engage him on the point."

"You let him get away with it?" Novak was lying on the left side of the bed, his feet facing the headboard while his head extended over the foot. Barbara supported him as he turned his face to the left, watching the edge of his father's portrait dance to the lower right of his vision. She often helped him perform this morning maneuver to combat vertigo.

"McMahon was trying to divert me from a more important point. I wouldn't let him." When she didn't respond, he said. "I understand where he's coming from. He's been doing this job for the past few months, holding things together, and figures he deserved the promotion. So he's testing me."

"Still, what makes him think he can speak to you like that?"

"That is an excellent question." He raised himself to a sitting position, then stood, steadying himself. It wouldn't be easy to fire McMahon without cause, and a bit of lip was insufficient grounds. Besides, he himself had been in the job less than a week and didn't want to risk alienating others on the force. He needed to earn their loyalty.

Still, Barbara's question was valid. What made McMahon think he could challenge Novak this early in their relationship?

"Better?" she said.

"Some. I may have to repeat it."

"Have you told your officers about this?"

"No," he said, his tone clipped. "I don't intend to."

"Is that wise? What if someone finds out?"

His grunted response could have meant anything, but she needed no translation.

"How would you feel about Father Murray coming for Sunday dinner?" Barbara said.

There was nothing subtle about her change in subject. Novak wondered how long she'd been waiting to introduce it. "No," he said.

"I take it you wouldn't be favorably disposed."

"Mother's idea?"

"She wants to have him over. And she lives here too, you know."

He sighed. "Yes, I do know. All right. Invite him. I'll make myself scarce."

"Karol."

"I'll go to the office. Or watch the Pirates lose."

"You hate baseball."

"Soccer, then. There's always a match somewhere."

She waved a hand in submission. "All right. I'll tell her not this time."

───────

THE VASCAR TEAM wrote only two tickets that Friday. Targeted enforcement was working. Novak spent his morning huddling with the borough's finance director. He hoped to boost morale by addressing maintenance issues at headquarters, but that line item was so small he couldn't buy so much as a can of rust remover.

The council wouldn't appreciate him asking for more money this early in his watch, but Barbara had told him the first six months would be the best time to get what he needed to do his job. He drafted a lengthy request and emailed it before the inner voice of caution could intrude.

He opened the locked filing cabinet and reviewed the personnel files of every officer. Many were veterans of the force and had served nowhere else, but there were exceptions.

Detective Horvath had started as a part-time officer with a township in the "Mon Valley," the depressed center of Pittsburgh's once-thriving steel industry.

Lydia Barnwell had earned a pre-law degree at Duquesne University, the Catholic institution overlooking the Monongahela River in Uptown Pittsburgh. After graduating cum laude, she'd breezed through the MPOBTP—the Municipal Police Officers' Basic Training Program—with outstanding marks. Then there'd been a gap. Upon earning Act 120 certification as a law officer, she'd applied to the Boyleston Police Department. And waited. Half a year had elapsed—had she spent the time applying to other agencies?—before the borough decided it might survive hiring its first female officer. Her file held no notices of disciplinary action, nor did it contain commendations. She was just *there*—a bureaucratic non-entity.

Sergeant Mayfield's career had followed a similar trajectory. After graduating from Pitt, he'd passed the MPOBTP. He'd waited a year for the borough to act on his application before enrolling in the Forensic Science and Law Program at Duquesne. Having earned a master's degree, he'd endured a long stretch of employment as a security guard before Boyleston hired him as a patrol officer. It had taken five years for him to make sergeant, despite applying twice for vacant positions. Again, no disciplinary record, but neither did Novak find commendations.

Laudatory testaments studded the records of half the other sergeants and patrolmen, but Chief Russell had ignored these two. Novak wrote a few words and highlighted both names in yellow.

He picked up another officer's file, and his note-taking became more animated. As he'd done for Barnwell and Mayfield, he calculated the intervals in the work history of this officer. But unlike their cases, in which he could picture months of fruitless searching for employment, he found no explanation for these gaps.

He penned a large question mark at the bottom of his page of notes, circling it with the highlighter. He resolved to learn more about the background of this member of his force.

———————

KAROL AND BARBARA returned from watching the Riverhounds' satisfying 1-0 victory over Atlanta at eleven o'clock. They were preparing for bed when the call came. Novak jumped into jeans and a T-shirt, slipping on loafers without socks, and dashed three-quarters of a mile to a convenience store on Powell that was owned by a man he knew.

A man who now lay dead on the floor behind his counter, a bullet hole where his left eye had been.

And Ajai Patel standing over the body of his brother, Aditya— Adi to his many friends—with tears streaming down his face as he moaned in a language unrecognizable to either Novak or Detective Mayfield.

Novak eased him away. "You need to leave him as he is, Ajai. We mustn't disturb evidence."

"Why?" the man cried. "We came to this country in peace. We treat everyone with respect and are honest with customers. Why would someone do this?"

"I don't know, Ajai, but I promise I'll find out."

He led the victim's brother to a patrol car. Dozens of bystanders crowded the periphery of the parking lot, which Officer Kimrey had blocked by stringing yellow tape between two cruisers and a lamppost.

"Have you informed his wife?" Novak asked.

"Priya, my wife, will tell her." Ajai looked up through rheumy eyes. "Please, sir, what happens now?"

Novak explained the procedure. The county police and crime lab were en route. After they finished taking photos, the coroner would examine the body before it was removed, Either Ajai or Saanvi, Adi's widow, would be asked to make a formal identification. The coroner would perform an autopsy. "The county will lead the investigation," he said, "but I assure you that our department will do everything possible to find Adi's killer."

Ajai nodded. "I have to go," Novak said. "My job starts now."

Despite his shock and grief, Patel honored the chief with a smile.

Novak returned to the store. "What do we know?" he asked Mayfield.

"Not much. Dispatch got a call at 11:35 from someone who didn't identify himself. The caller said he needed gas and saw the lights still on, so he pulled in. He knew Patel always closed at eleven, so after filling his tank, he got curious. He walked in, found Patel lying behind the counter, and called 9-1-1 from the store's phone. He didn't stick around and wouldn't leave a name."

"If he gassed up, he had to have used his credit card, which will make it easy to find him," Novak said. "Any other witnesses?"

"None that I know of. I arrived a few minutes before you. Kimrey was first on the scene, and the lot was empty. Once passers-by saw his flashing lights..." He left the thought unfinished.

"So we're unsure whether it's the same person responsible for the other robberies?"

Mayfield shook his head.

"Did you notify McMahon?"

"Yes." In answer to Novak's questioning gaze, he added, "He didn't respond."

The first county cruiser arrived, followed by a second. Novak introduced his men and summarized what little they had learned. The county patrolmen helped Kimrey maintain security until homicide detectives and the crime lab arrived.

"How did Ajai get here so fast?" Novak said.

"He was closing his store when he saw Kimrey running Code 3. He sensed what had happened and followed him. He told me, 'I just knew.'"

"It's the same guy," he told Barbara three hours later as they lay alongside each other in bed. "We viewed the CCTV footage. It's him, right down to his blue trainers."

Novak and his team had watched multiple scenes from cameras placed above the register, at the rear of the store, at both ends of the pumps, and at the east and west approaches. Rather than handing over the cash, Patel had argued with the man and, when he pulled a weapon from the left pocket of his oversized jacket, lunged over the counter to grab it. The flash wasn't visible from the camera angle, but as Patel fell back, a trace of smoke issued from the barrel.

The robber—the killer, now—had stared at his gun and at Patel, then turned without touching the cash register. An exterior camera had shown him running west from the lot, downhill on Powell. As he'd disappeared from view, all officers had turned from the screen, all except Sergeant Mayfield, who'd called them back seconds later. "Catch this."

The west-facing camera had shown a figure on a motor scooter heading uphill on Powell. The east-facing camera had recorded the two-wheeler as it continued up the avenue and swung left out of the frame. "South on Hawthorne," Mayfield had said, "toward the river."

Novak had clapped him on the shoulder. County Detective Sergeant Glen Carpenter had issued a grudging, "Nice work." Perhaps they had something to go on.

"You knew him," Barbara said.

"I often gas up there. It's a typical immigrant story. His cousin moved here first, worked hard, got some help from his family in India to buy a convenience store. Once he paid it off, he sent for Ajai. He came over and worked for the cousin for a while, borrowed money from home to buy his own shop, then sent for Adi. All of them virtually live on-site, starting each morning at seven, working through the whole day, closing at eleven, catching a few hours' sleep, then returning early the next morning. Same routine, day after day, seven days a week, fifty-two weeks a year. Honest, hard-working men, devoted to their families, and this is what they get."

Novak studied the ceiling, reliving what he'd seen. "I had a bad feeling about this all week. I was sure he'd strike again, that it would lead to something like this."

Barbara rubbed his shoulder. "When we were first married and you were a patrolman, I lay awake every night worrying that you wouldn't come home, that I'd never see you again. When Jerry Sprague was killed, we sat behind Alice at the funeral. We sat alongside Marquesa Washington at Clarence's service. For years, I lived in constant fear."

He turned toward her, and she curled up in his arm. "When you made detective, I was relieved at first. You were off the street. Out of harm's way. But then I worried that the job would make you jaded, that you'd start looking at everyone as a potential criminal."

"It happens to a lot of us," he said.

"So when you retired, I relaxed. I could finally stop worrying. But I could tell you were unhappy. When this opportunity came up, I was all for it, thought it would allow you to find a purpose. But now," she said, "I worry again."

"The life of a cop's wife," he said. "I'm careful. I promise to come back in one piece. But I must get this guy."

Barbara disengaged from him and turned off the bedside lamp. They lay awake for another quarter hour, neither speaking. He thought she had gone to sleep and was about to drift off himself when he muttered something.

She sat up. "What did you say?"

"Hmm? I'm wondering where she came up with this wish."

She followed his conversational leap. "Someone in the family, I suppose."

"You told me that when Amy blurted it out, Bridey was angry with her. I doubt it was a topic of conversation around their dinner table. How did she find out? What made it suddenly so important to her?"

Barbara turned on the lamp, rested on her left elbow, and smoothed his hair with her right. "Someone else told her. Her brother. A cousin."

"And how did she connect it to me? The council had appointed me only two nights before."

"That's easy," Barbara said. "A parent told a child who told a classmate, and by the end of school Friday, everyone knew that Jen's pap is the new police chief. If you think that's unusual, you're not paying enough attention to your own nine-year-old archetype. They're all like her."

"We need to find out why she became so curious about it. Would you talk with her?"

"I'm not allowed to probe the private lives of kids—even those in another school—unless there's an educational issue or evidence of abuse. You're the cop."

"And I can't get involved. I'm new, it was never our case, and with this homicide, we're overwhelmed. No, no way."

BARBARA LAY awake until her husband dozed off, his deep breathing signaling he would soon begin to snore. She turned off the light and rolled him onto his side, then tucked herself between the sheets.

Only then did she allow herself a smile of contentment. She knew him. No matter what he said, he was hooked. She didn't need to pull on the line. He would reel himself in.

ADITYA PATEL

CHAPTER FOUR
TAKE CARE OF YOUR PEOPLE

N ovak spent Sunday at headquarters, while his mother took his place alongside Barbara at the Pittsburgh Symphony's performance of the Verdi Requiem with the full Mendelssohn Choir. He regretted missing it, but Patel's slaying took precedence.

Alongside Mayfield and Horvath, he spent hours reviewing videos and descriptions from all three robberies and combing records of past holdups for connections that could produce leads. On Monday morning, Novak assembled the entire department to share what they'd learned and to map their approach.

"We've had three armed robberies within two weeks," he said. "The same person committed them, and the victims were members of the same family, immigrants from a state in western India. We don't know if there's a racial or ethnic angle to this, but we can't discount it.

"The first two came off without incident when the owners handed over their cash. But Saturday night, Aditya Patel resisted. He has two young kids, a third on the way. He is still repaying a business loan from his family back in India, so he may have felt he had more to lose."

"And he certainly did," Mark Ewer piped up. He looked around as though pleased with himself, but encountered only silence.

Extending the hush, Novak let the chill envelop the loquacious detective before continuing. "As you can see from the photos, he wears baggy jeans, a jacket that hangs down to his knees in which he conceals the weapon, a gray baseball cap with the word 'Shiner' on it, whatever that means—"

"It's a Texas beer," Barnwell said. "Very popular there."

Novak raised his eyebrows. "Thank you. Everyone note that, please. There may be a connection. He wears lightweight plastic gloves, the kind often used in restaurants. We don't know how significant that may be, but we're paying attention to it. He pulls a sheer net over his face to distort his features—a length of pantyhose, perhaps—"

That brought a snicker from Ewer, which Novak ignored. "He's clean-shaven. One victim thought he might be Asian, but given the disguise, we can't rely on that."

"I haven't seen those used in years," McMahon said. "They normally go for ski masks."

Novak was glad to have his deputy, who'd been silent up to that point, chime in. "I agree, but a full face mask is visible to any passerby, whereas a stocking is evident only at close range."

"And evenings are getting warm."

"Right. Very good." He nodded at McMahon.

"Thanks to Sergeant Mayfield, we also know he makes his getaway on a motor scooter." He pressed the remote, and the still image of the killer changed to a video.

"Here he is leaving the scene of Saturday night's shooting." He let both videos run. "And here he is arriving at the first robbery on Walnut two weeks ago."

"Is it a Vespa, or—"

"We don't know," Horvath answered. "We've had an expert enlarge and enhance every frame, but the scooter's a long ways away, moving at high speed, and the lens was wide open at night, blurring the edges." Novak nodded. Horvath had impressed him the afternoon before with his knowledge of photography.

"From this distance and in this light," the detective continued, "we're not even sure of the color. It appears to be light green, but that might be a reflection of traffic lights. We just can't tell."

"While the county has the lead on this, he has murdered a citizen of this borough." Novak slammed both fists on the table before him and scanned every face. "So we will find this bastard."

HORVATH HANDED OUT ASSIGNMENTS. Half the patrol officers would fan out across the borough, sharing surveillance photos of the suspect with business owners. They would concentrate first on restaurants and bars. The other half, working in teams of two, would knock on doors in The Shanties and in apartments that offered Section 8 housing. If necessary, they would work their way up the economic ladder the following week.

The three detectives would split up. Ewer would continue to identify similarities to past robberies while Horvath and Mayfield searched mug shots and records of recently released felons. The chief would make the rounds of motorcycle sales and repair shops.

Mayfield had found a recent robbery in neighboring Dormont that resembled the Boyleston cases, so Novak called Martin Stansell, Dormont's chief, whom he knew from cross-jurisdictional investigations during his years with Pittsburgh Police. Stansell congratulated him on his appointment. Having read the report of Adi Patel's murder, he had already stepped up evening patrols around convenience stores in his borough.

Novak gave him the subject's description and means of transportation. "We first wondered if he was using a moped because his driver's license is suspended, but that makes no sense."

"Yeah, like a perp willing to commit multiple armed robberies would worry about driving with an expired license. What's your next theory?"

"We have two. One is that he can't afford a car, or his has broken down."

Stansell was unconvinced. Anyone bold enough to rob stores was equally capable of stealing cars.

"More likely, he's just canny," Novak said. "Back streets criss-cross all the boroughs, some so narrow it's hard to drive through them except at a crawl. Whereas a motorbike or a scooter—"

"Maneuverability," Stansell said. "If he's pursued, he can pull into a space between garages or hide behind them. Makes sense."

"One more thing. The suspect wore the kind of light plastic gloves used by food service workers. Our officers are talking to owners of delis, bars, and restaurants. If you can spare the manpower, I'd appreciate your doing the same."

Stansell whistled. "You've got it. We figure he's committed three robberies here, and Pittsburgh has him for a pair in Brookline. He's making a path across the South Hills."

Why didn't we know this?

The answer was not long in coming.

"We're glad you've taken command. Not just me. The chiefs of other boroughs. We've had little cooperation on any case for months."

Given the glut of jurisdictions across the county, inter-agency coordination was essential to law enforcement. He asked Stansell for specifics.

"There's been little sharing of other than essential information. Never any outreach. When we ask for help, it's given grudgingly, if at all. They're always 'kind of busy here.' We've found it best to go around your deputy. Horvath and Ewer are okay, but Mayfield is our go-to guy."

Asking Stansell to hold on, Novak closed his office door. He probed to make sure he was directing his frustration primarily at McMahon.

"I'm not trying to get him in trouble," Stansell said. "My sense is he's been running the place single-handedly for at least a year. I didn't understand what the problem was until Russell's arrest. He left everything to McMahon."

Thanking him, Novak called Charlie Watson, who'd taken his

place as chief of detectives in Pittsburgh. Watson was less forthcoming. No cop likes to betray another, and it was only due to their personal relationship that Watson told him what he needed to know.

"I dealt with the department for years when I was at your desk," Novak said. "I never had a problem."

Watson hesitated a moment. "It didn't become an issue until about eighteen months ago, about the time you...left."

"WHERE'S MCMAHON?" Novak strolled through the department looking for his deputy chief and finally put the question to the dispatcher.

"He left about a quarter hour ago," she said. "He didn't sign out."

"He drives the blue Galaxy, doesn't he?" She nodded. It was still in the parking lot.

He poked his head into offices once more, rechecked the men's room, and accepted the fact that McMahon was not in this wing.

But he might be in the building. He could be in the library, but Novak had a hunch he wasn't into recreational reading. Passing through the connecting door, he entered the administrative wing and made a show of greeting each person he encountered.

Only one office door was closed. "The mayor in?" he asked the assistant.

"Yes," she said. "He's in a meeting."

"With the deputy chief?"

"Yes. Shall I tell him you're looking for him?"

"Sure," Novak said. "Let him know I came by."

"I HATE THE POLITICS," Novak told Barbara that evening. Izabela had made *halupki*, stuffed cabbage rolls, which she'd served with boiled potatoes. While she sat in the living room watching Wheel of

Fortune at peak volume, the two cleaned up, closing the swinging kitchen door to hear each other.

"I didn't have to deal with this crap at the bureau. Someone did, probably the chief, but not me."

Novak related his conversations with his Dormont and Pittsburgh colleagues, as well as his discovery of McMahon's tête-à-tête with Mayor Tifton. "I was trying to hit the reset button. We got off to a bad start, and Stansell speculated he's borne the responsibility for the department longer than anyone realized. As soon as I got off the phone, I went looking for him to say I understand what he's gone through and want us to work together. All the time I paraded around holding an olive branch, the SOB was meeting with Tifton, violating my specific instructions."

Barbara smiled and touched his arm. "You don't know what they were discussing."

"It makes no difference. I told him all borough communications are to go through me."

"I understand, but it may have been social. Just remember, you have full retirement from the city. You don't need this."

"But I do need it."

"You need to stay active. You don't want to be buried at fifty-six. I get that. But you don't need *this*. The borough, on the other hand, needs *you*. It's a screwed-up operation, they don't pay well, they want stability, and you were the only candidate with the experience to take this on. They need you more than you need them."

He kept drying a plate until she took it from him. "I'll keep that in mind."

Grabbing a clean towel, he turned to the pile of pots and pans his mother had managed to soil as Barbara finished washing them. "It's why I keep you around," he said.

"All this time I thought it was just for sex."

"That, too."

The telephone interrupted their colloquy before they could

pursue the matter upstairs. Novak listened, asked a few questions, and said, "I'll be there."

"That," he said as he hung up, "was Councilman Jackson. He wants to meet me in the morning."

"What about?"

"He didn't say, but he doesn't want others to know, so he's set it for a little diner in Carnegie."

"Which reminds me, Jen called this afternoon. She asked what you've learned about Amy's grandfather. I gather her friend is pestering her."

"Did you explain I can't do that?"

"No, I said I'd ask you."

"Thanks." He didn't conceal his annoyance. "This isn't Pittsburgh, where we had our own crime technicians, forensics lab, and homicide detectives. Boyleston has none of that. That's why we hand homicides and crimes of violence off to the county. The Walsh case was never ours."

She reached across the sink, stroking his arm, peering into his eyes. "You know how Jen looks up to you. She thinks her pap can do anything."

"We have to bring down Adi's killer before he hurts anyone else. It's all that matters right now."

"I understand. But can you take a quick look? Satisfy yourself that they didn't overlook anything back then? If not..." When he didn't respond, she added, "For your granddaughter?"

With a sigh loud enough to be heard over the blaring TV, he said, "All right. But she shouldn't expect anything, because I doubt there's anything to find."

———

NOVAK ARRIVED at the diner first, parking himself at a table near the front window where he could watch the street. He ordered coffee, toying with the packets of sugar while he waited. Bernie Jackson followed five minutes later. He flagged down the waitress and ordered eggs, hash browns, sausage, and a banana. Novak had already had breakfast, so he contented himself with yogurt and "fresh fruit," which, it developed, might once have been fresh before being stuffed into a can.

Jackson thanked him for coming and poured two packets of ersatz cream into his coffee while studying Novak over the rim of his glasses. He was a handsome man, cocoa-colored skin contrasting with light gray hair and an unlined face that belied his sixty-plus years. Novak had known him for as long as he could remember, but so had most people in the borough. Jackson owned a local portrait studio and had taken the yearbook photos of everyone passing through Boyleston High School—charging nothing to kids whose parents couldn't afford his already-modest rates. Whenever a White person in Boyleston disavowed any racist tendency by proclaiming that they had a Black friend, they were referring to Bernie.

Novak briefed him on the armed robberies and the steps he was taking. "Adi was a sweet guy," the councilman said. "Tireless worker, devoted to his family. It turns my stomach."

They spent a few minutes reminiscing about the man and his extended family.

"It sounds like you have things well in hand," Jackson said, "but that's not why I called."

Novak remained silent, suspecting Jackson would explain the reason for his summons. "I want to apologize."

"What for?"

"For voting against you."

Novak waved it away with his hand. "There's no need."

"Yes, there is. It wasn't personal; it had nothing to do with you. I was protesting the fact that Sergeant Mayfield didn't make the cut."

The waitress slid the plate in front of him, but Jackson ignored it. "And not because he's Black. I don't operate that way. I can't afford to, nor do I want to. I was protesting the fact that Mayfield wasn't a finalist *because* he was Black."

Jackson paused to make certain Novak caught the distinction. "Have you looked at his resumé?"

"I have. It's impressive. He worked hard to get where he is."

"Sergeant Mayfield is the best-educated person on the force, including you. He has a master's degree in criminology. Education isn't everything, but he should have had a shot." Jackson stopped speaking while he shoveled food into his mouth. He cleaned his plate, ran his napkin across his mustache, and wiped his hands on it. "You impress me."

Novak frowned, shook his head, and extended his left hand, palm up.

"Standing up to Frain," Jackson said, as though Novak had posed the question out loud. "Ending the practice of writing off tickets. That's courageous."

"I don't look at it that way. I need to establish sound practices. When I see something wrong, I put a stop to it, rather than letting it drift on for a month or two."

Jackson nodded agreement.

"It didn't take long for word to get around," Novak said.

"Frain called me before Noon Friday, and I doubt I was the first to hear about it. He's angry. Few people tell him no."

Novak rotated his empty coffee cup, which was advertised as bottomless. "Do you mind my asking you about Tifton?" The councilman signaled him to go ahead.

He related the dismissive way in which the mayor had introduced him to his officers the week before, his inference that Novak was merely a caretaker, and his closed-door meeting with Novak's deputy. "I suspect he's using McMahon as a conduit to keep tabs on me."

"Why do you think that?"

"Experience. I know what two and two equal."

Jackson sighed and stared past Novak. "Tifton may be trouble. He'd manipulated Chief Russell for years, making him ignore whatever might reflect badly on the borough. His boosterism clouds his judgment. He was less concerned about how Russell was ripping off the town than he was about the adverse publicity generated by his arrest. In the aftermath, Tifton wanted to put McMahon in his place. Maybe he thought he could manage him like he did Russell."

Jackson covered his mouth with his left hand as he used a right fingernail as a toothpick. "He's angry because you don't report to him," he continued. "We couldn't just do business as usual after seeing how poorly he'd supervised Russell. The council was forced to assume oversight of the police department. Tifton doesn't like it."

"Who would?" Novak said.

"As I said, his chief concern is promoting the borough. He wants Boyleston to return to the way it used to be—a working-class community with an upper-middle-class group of overseers, well-paying jobs for everyone, healthy commerce, lots of young, Catholic couples turning out children. He doesn't like how Boyleston's fortunes have declined. Not that anyone does—the decaying housing, loss of jobs, and all. I applaud his enthusiasm, but we can't let PR dictate everything we do."

Jackson waited to see if Novak would respond, but the experienced interrogator knew that silence was often just as productive as a question. "The police scandal, for instance," Jackson continued. "If he could have covered it up to protect Boyleston's reputation, I think he would have."

Novak raised his eyebrows.

"I don't want you repeating any of this."

"Of course not. I appreciate your candor."

"So now," Jackson said, "he's doing what he should have done all along—looking over your shoulder to make sure nothing like it happens again. And he's still trying to exert the authority he's lost. Just remember—you report to us, not to him."

Meanwhile, I'm caught in the middle.

Jackson picked up the check, telling the server she looked "damned cute today." Novak cringed until she told him he looked pretty good himself. He'd probably taken her high school photos, and those of her parents. Old friends.

"One more thing," he said as they stood outside the diner. "Your officers have been through a lot. They're demoralized. Most of them are good people. They'd be hard to replace, so treat them well."

CHAPTER FIVE
WHO WILL TELL HER?

Assailed by the moldy odor the moment he entered the station, Novak cursed himself for not raising his funding request with Jackson over breakfast. He would have to deal with Byron Frain, who chaired the budget committee, instead.

But that would have to come later. His officers had assembled in the bullpen, awaiting him. "Apologies. My meeting ran over." He offered no further explanation.

Horvath called on each team leader. The patrol officers working bars and restaurants had covered all but three, which were closed Mondays. One officer would return to them as soon as they opened at eleven while the others canvassed other businesses.

The team working residences had only begun. Ewer had found three similar holdups from past years, two of which had been solved. Of those, one convict remained in jail while the other was under five-six and Black. In the unsolved case, the suspect's description still didn't match. The detectives had come up empty.

Officer Barnwell spoke up. "Are we covering retirement homes and senior centers?"

Ewer whinnied, while McMahon whispered something to Horvath that Novak couldn't make out.

"They provide food services to their clients, just like restaurants," she told Ewer.

"Great idea," Novak said. "You take that on. And don't neglect small, home-based independent living facilities." There were dozens of them, making this a difficult task, but Novak admired her for picking up on a possibility he had overlooked.

He described his meeting with Chief Stansell, emphasizing that his department would question restaurant owners and managers in Dormont.

"We're putting a lot of stock in a pair of plastic gloves anyone could buy at Giant Eagle," McMahon said. "It's a thin reed."

"This and the motorbike are all we know," Novak said, concealing his own misgivings. "Unless you have a better idea."

McMahon shrugged, his expression blank.

"Even if we're only tossing stones in the water, the ripples may reveal something. If our guy doesn't work in a diner, he may eat there. Someone has to have seen something."

"But spending time on old folks' homes?"

"They're the one business we haven't considered. We're covering everything."

He waited for McMahon to renew his challenge and, hearing none, said, "All right. Let's get back to work. I want this guy."

NOVAK RETURNED to his office to find a file folder containing a report on the death of Rebecca Walsh, written by a retired borough detective by the name of Anthony Grico. He had worked with Grico years before on cross-jurisdictional cases and remembered him as a by-the-book professional.

The report had not been signed out in twenty years. Dated May 20, 1989, Grico reported being called to a residence on Spalding Street at 7:12 a.m.

Florence O'Rourke reported that the child of a neighbor, Bridey Walsh, appeared at her door shortly before seven o'clock. She said the child was crying and shivering and wore only a nightgown. At first, Mrs. O'Rourke couldn't make out what the little girl was saying. Then she understood that her mother, Rebecca Walsh, was ill.

Her husband, Terrence O'Rourke, crossed the street to investigate. On returning minutes later, he had her call Boyleston Police. Dispatcher Lois Grimaldi logged the call at 7:03 a.m. I had just arrived at the station and drove the eight blocks to the O'Rourke's address at 784 Spalding Street.

After speaking with Mr. O'Rourke, I entered the residence across the street at 789 Spalding Street. The front door was open. The child had not closed it when she went for help. I climbed the stairway to the second floor and entered the master bedroom to the right at the top of the stairs.

Inside, I found the body of a woman lying on the left side of the double bed. Her body was face up. A plastic bag covered her head, secured around her neck by industrial tape. The victim's hands were bound behind her using what appeared to be the same kind of tape. Her nightgown was up to her shoulders, revealing her breasts. Her panties were pulled down on her hips, just covering her pubic area. Facial bruises indicated that she may have been struck.

I checked the remaining rooms to make certain there were no individuals present. I returned to my patrol car and directed our dispatcher to notify Allegheny County Police of a homicide. After securing the house, I called Child Protective Services to take charge of the girl.

Grico's report described Allegheny County Police Detective Andrew Millar's arrival, followed by the county crime lab, and his attempts to question neighbors about anything they had seen or heard during the nighttime hours. He'd had little success, since many were

up and around on a warm spring Saturday. He recommended that
the county conduct more thorough interviews.

Terrence O'Rourke told him the victim's husband, Thomas
Walsh, had gone fishing with friends for the weekend. He reported
they were at Bessemer Lake in Lawrence County, sixty miles north of
Boyleston near the Ohio border. With the approval of Detective
Millar, Grico notified the Lawrence County Sheriff's Office, which
sent a deputy to the boat ramp.

> They located Mr. Walsh and notified him that his wife had been
> found dead. Lawrence County Deputy Michael Garvey reported
> Mr. Walsh was so distraught that one of his companions had to
> drive him home. When he arrived, the ACPD questioned him.
>
> I had no further involvement in the investigation, as it comes
> under the jurisdiction of the ACPD.

Novak reread the report and made several notes. He returned the
file to Norma Showalter, asking her to make a copy and determine if
the retired detective was still alive and living in the area. She looked
up at him, glanced in both directions, seemed about to speak, but
stopped.

"What is it?"

"It's just..." She paused as though uncertain whether to speak.
Novak waited. "The deputy chief asked me why you were looking at
that file."

"What did you tell him?"

"That I don't know."

Novak smiled. "Right answer. Nice work."

"WE DIDN'T BUDGET for physical maintenance." Councilman Frain
turned away, as though the conversation was over.

"I understand that," Novak said. "I'm requesting emergency funding."

"It's hardly an emergency." A tight-lipped smile.

"Have you visited the public safety wing recently? The walls are a patchwork of peeling paint. The place stinks of mildew." He forced himself to lower his voice. "The atmosphere is demoralizing and unhealthy."

"We draw up next year's budget in October. Put your request in then."

Novak sighed, his eyes circling the councilman's office. "I'll transfer money from the training budget to cover minimal improvements."

Frain was obdurate. "Some of that is federal funding. You can't go moving money from one line item to the next."

"Another fund, then?"

For the first time in their brief conversation, Frain looked directly at him. "Judge Magnotti dismissed my ticket."

Novak's confusion was only momentary. "I'm not surprised." *Woody Allen's observation also applies to beating a traffic ticket. Eighty percent of success is showing up.*

"Fortunately, she believes in justice," Frain said.

"That's her job. I have mine."

"And what do you think that is?"

"It's my duty to enforce the law without fear or favor. Justice is up to the court."

"You're one of those what-have-you-done-for-me-lately types. That's not how we operate. If you expect the council to be flexible, bend a little yourself. Understand?"

"Oh," Novak said, "do I. But as long as I'm chief, I'll do my duty." He turned and left.

By the end of the week, they'd made no progress in identifying Patel's killer. The patrol officers had covered every business in town. The house-to-house search had turned up nothing. Novak had visited every scooter dealer and called every independent repair shop south of the Monongahela River. Detective Ewer had searched the records for stolen mopeds. Despite all their work, they knew no more than they had Monday morning.

Late Friday afternoon, McMahon sauntered into his office. "The men don't like this. We're chasing our tails and getting nowhere. They want back on their beats."

Choosing not to point out that the department didn't use a beat system, Novak said, "We'll keep at it for another few days. The mere act of questioning landlords and business owners keeps this in the public eye. We're more likely to get a break if we create it."

McMahon snorted and left. *So much for your leadership skills, Deputy.*

Novak checked the police docket—a knife attack the previous night at a local bar, a two-car accident with injuries on the main road into Pittsburgh during morning rush hour, and a purse-snatching in full view of witnesses on Mason Drive at Noon. All under control.

He checked out, telling Norma Showalter he had an appointment. Since she had provided Anthony Grico's phone number and address at the start of the day, he presumed she knew where he was headed. The retired detective lived in Peters Township, an upscale ex-urban community in neighboring Washington County thirty miles south of Boyleston. Novak pulled in front of a two-story Colonial on Maltese Lane, which was off Collie Court, off Cocker Avenue. He couldn't believe a hard-boiled cop had traded the gritty streets and alleys of Boyleston for a neighborhood that was so—he searched for the right word—*fey.*

Grico opened the door before he rang, the burly, silver-haired Italian looking older but otherwise unchanged from the last time they'd worked together. "Come on in. Have any trouble finding the place?"

Novak extolled the virtues of GPS, but Grico seemed not to listen as he led the way into a large family room with windows overlooking a treed yard filled with playground equipment. "Seven grandkids," he said, swooping his hand. "How did they rope you into taking this job? I thought you'd retired."

"You've heard about Chief Russell?"

"Yeah." A derisive laugh. "We get TV news even out here in the sticks. Running a security business using borough cops, cars, and gear. Sent out invoices under a company called Boyleston Police Services or something like that. Didn't he also lift some equipment?"

"We've recovered some of it, but not all."

"And he'll do time."

"He reached a plea deal to avoid trial. He's doing two years at SCI Somerset," Novak said, referring to the state correctional institution southeast of Pittsburgh.

"Inmates always give an ex-cop a rough time." Grico shook his head. "Jason always was a stupid shit. He only got the job because he did what the mayor—what's his name?"

"Fred Tifton."

"Tifton, yeah. Russell did as he was told. Played by the mayor's rules. Didn't make waves. Or so he thought." Novak muttered agreement. "Hey, you want something to drink? A beer?"

"Ice water is fine."

"On duty, are we?"

Novak didn't answer.

"So, what brings you all the way out here?" Grico returned from the kitchen carrying a plastic Pirates commemorative cup filled with ice water.

"The Rebecca Walsh murder. You were first on the scene. I read your report." He handed Grico a copy. "To the point. If you want a post-retirement job, you can teach my officers how to write reports." Grico chuckled, but waved away the suggestion.

"I'm interested in what happened after you handed it off to the county," Novak said.

He looked over his old account of the murder before speaking. "This was long ago, What's changed?"

"Maybe nothing. A citizen asked me to review it."

"And you have time for this?" Grico stared at the brocade pattern on the ceiling as though he'd find another page of the report projected onto its surface. "Matt Harris was the investigating officer. Remember him? Gone now. Pancreatic cancer. Forty-nine years old."

"Your report lists Andy Millar as the first on the scene."

"Yeah." He studied the ceiling again. "Millar was there first, but Harris must have outranked him, because he was in charge from the moment he sized it up."

Harris' name seemed familiar. Had Novak worked with him?

Grico grimaced, wrinkled his nose as though at a foul odor, and shook his head. "The husband, Thomas Walsh, was a local business-man, owned a hardware store in Boyleston, churchgoing, pillar of the community and all that. It was Memorial Day weekend. He'd gone fishing at Bessemer Lake with three buddies. Saturday morning, their daughter discovered the mother's body and ran to a neighbor. The neighbor entered the house and found her lying in bed, suffocated. You got all that from the report."

"What happened then?"

"We alerted the Bessemer PD, who reported back that while Walsh's three buddies spent the night together at the lakeside lodge, Walsh was off by himself. His buddies said he'd always stayed with them. Walsh had some bullshit explanation—they drank too much, and he was trying to quit. Some excuse like that. But it was out of character and meant no one could confirm his alibi for the night."

Novak saw Grico eyeing his notepad as he scribbled. "There was no sign of forced entry," Grico said. "After making the ninety-minute drive back to Boyleston, Walsh could have unlocked the front door, walked in, and suffocated her. His prints were all over the house and the bedroom, but he lived there, so that was no big deal. His buddies had driven him back to town, so the county recovered his car at the lake. They found a box of plastic bags and a roll of duct tape in the trunk. His face was scratched, and he claimed he'd walked into a tree branch. He was looking guilty."

"Wasn't there some scandal," Novak said, "a girlfriend?"

"Not him, her. She'd been seeing some guy on the side. She was pregnant, but he'd told a friend they were having problems and hadn't had sex in months. I don't think they ever found the boyfriend, but it gave Walsh a motive. He flunked a polygraph test. They charged him with her murder. He denied everything for a while but finally confessed."

Grico leaned forward and ran both hands through his silver hair, as though trying to coax the memory from his head. "It was a plea deal. He confessed to avoid the death penalty. The trial was perfunctory. He was found guilty. Later he recanted and started filing appeals, but he'd blabbed to a cellmate, admitting he'd killed her. Can't remember all the details. Last I heard, Walsh is still at the supermax facility in Greene."

"You have a good memory."

"It was the worst case I was ever involved in, even though the county took the lead. You don't forget that sort of thing."

"Did you ever question his guilt?"

"Walsh?" He exploded with laughter. "Never. Does this citizen of yours claim he's innocent? Don't waste your time, Karol. Means, motive, opportunity. I know it's seldom that simple, but he had all three, plus abundant physical evidence. He killed her all right."

MARIEL BROUGHT Jennifer to the house after Sunday Mass. With the temperature nearing seventy, Novak and his granddaughter kicked a soccer ball back and forth for a quarter hour. Barbara and Mariel watched the pair shout with delight.

Suddenly, Novak straightened up, rubbing his temples with the fingers of both hands. Jen nutmegged him and shouted, "Go-o-o-oal!"

Mariel rose from her chair, Barbara close behind her. "Are you okay, Dad?"

He stood still for a few seconds. "Just tired, that's all. Your mom and I scrubbed down the walls of the cop shop yesterday. Jen, let's stop for a few minutes."

"Aw-w-w. And I was winning."

"Jen, leave your pap alone for a minute."

Novak sank into a lawn chair while his wife and daughter looked on in concern. After a few minutes, he got to his feet and fired up the gas grill. He cooked hamburgers for the adults and a hot dog for Jen, while Barbara prepared a salad and Izabela produced her ubiquitous *halusky* from the refrigerator.

Over lunch, Izabela gave her rendition of Father Murray's homily, which described what happened to lambs who strayed from the flock.

"Didn't he give the same message last week?" Novak said.

"Did he?" She took another helping of the cheese-and-potato dish.

Barbara aimed a kick at his ankle but connected with the leg of the patio table instead. She stifled an outcry. "Summer's on the way," she said to cover her mishap. "Smell those lilacs!"

The only thing Novak smelled was his mother's weekly attempt to get him back to Mass. Barbara and Mariel dominated the rest of the luncheon, grousing at the school board's proposed budget, which called for layoffs of teachers and administrative staff. As the conversation grew heated, Izabela reminded them that "little people have big ears."

Only when their little person wandered off in pursuit of a fledged cardinal did Novak share his conclusion. "I looked into the Walsh murder. I've read our reports and spoken to the officer who first responded. There seems to be no question that Thomas Walsh killed his wife."

He described the investigation, the evidence, and the unsuccessful appeal to the governor for clemency. "So the questions become: who explains this to young Amy, and how they do it."

They met him with silence. "I can't speak to her without her mother's permission."

"Neither can I," Barbara said.

Mariel also bowed out, despite Jen's friendship with Amy. "I'm not *her* teacher, but I am *a* teacher, and I can't drag a nine-year-old child aside to discuss her grandmother's murder. It's against the rules...and it isn't right."

"Then we have to go through Bridey."

"Which won't be easy," Mariel said. "She's a piece of work. You should see how she treats that child."

The way she said it told Novak everything he needed to know about why Mariel had taken Amy under her wing. She wasn't just Jen's friend. She was a wounded bird.

In the end, Mariel agreed to ask Bridey O'Connor's permission for Novak to meet with her and her daughter.

"There's just one thing," Barbara said. "You met with your officer, but you keep reminding me it was the county's case. Shouldn't you speak to them?"

Novak took a deep breath. "No, and I'm not going to. I have no reason to reopen this. There's no sign anything was amiss with the investigation, the lead detective is dead, and Walsh confessed. Case closed. I've focused all available resources on solving Patel's murder."

"But, Karol..."

He placed his hand on her arm and looked into her eyes. "Barbara, I've done what I can. The answer is no."

CHAPTER SIX
PRESSURE COOKER

Novak ended each evening by reviewing his notes from the day. He underlined things he found important, highlighted names he needed to remember, and committed what was important to memory. On weekends, he reviewed these highlights, listing what he needed to accomplish during the coming week, people with whom he should meet, and subjects for further investigation.

While Barbara watched *Masterpiece* on Sunday evening, he reviewed his conversation with Tony Grico. As he read a name, a memory flashed across his consciousness, then burned out like a meteor. Something about Grico's manner during that part of the conversation told him he was missing something. He made a note to research the name and recover the memory.

His cell phone rang. Detective Horvath. He listened for a moment, took down an address, and tore from the house. He arrived at the residence on Farmington Avenue within minutes. Two borough patrol cars blocked the street, an ambulance stood out front, and, as Novak pulled up, an unmarked county car pulled in behind him.

The house was a two-story frame dwelling with white vinyl siding, reflecting the blue and red pulses of the ambulance and squad cars. Neighbors, some in pajamas and robes, stood on either side of the yellow crime scene tape that blocked the sidewalk. A steep hill opposite the house prevented more spectators from gawking.

Horvath met him on the narrow porch and waited until the county officer joined them. "Irene Matola," he said. "Thirty-nine. Husband, Frank, beat her senseless. Still alive, but..."

Two ambulance attendants emerged, wheeling a gurney. The officers stepped off the narrow porch while they passed. A sheet covered the victim's head. A tube protruded from the edge and led to a machine attached to one end. The attendants dropped the wheels as they descended the stairs, wheeled the victim to the street, slid the gurney into the ambulance, closed the door, and left. Their siren sang a mournful wail as the colored strobes retreated down the avenue toward US 19 and Mercy Hospital's trauma center.

Horvath led the two county detectives into the house, Novak trailing behind. In the living room, Frank Matola sat on a sofa whose guts spilled out like a hernia. His knuckles were bruised and bleeding, and his long-sleeve T-shirt, bearing the name and logo of a local brew pub, was splattered with what appeared to be bloodstains. He was a small man, perhaps five-seven, with a thin frame, wan complexion, and fine, tousled hair in full retreat from his forehead. His most distinctive features were his eyes—set deep in his face and the darkest brown Novak had seen in a White man. He looked up as they entered, his puzzled expression like that of a small child wondering what the adults expected of him.

A county detective—Sanchez, Novak later learned—asked him to identify himself and said, "Can you tell me what happened?"

"She wouldn't stop," Matola said in a hoarse treble voice. "She kept nagging me, harassing me. I warned her. I really did, but she kept whining. I put an end to it."

"You hit her," Sanchez said.

"Slapped her, just enough to shut her up."

"But you hit her?"

Matola nodded. "She'll be all right. She's faking again to grab attention."

Before the detective could respond, they heard a shriek from outside the house. "That bastard! He's done it again! The bastard!"

Officer Kimrey entered the house, red-faced, fingering his hat, wiping his forehead with his sleeve. "Someone'd better come talk to this woman. She insists on speaking to whoever's in charge."

Novak followed Kimrey outside. Officer Barnwell was struggling to restrain a woman with flaming red hair and a body fifty pounds too heavy for her form-fitting exercise outfit, and who was blaring a string of invective.

He introduced himself. The woman continued screaming. He tried again. She stopped in mid-cry, aimed a painted fingernail at him. "You!"

Novak waited.

"You let this happen! She wanted to press charges, but you told her not to."

Novak took a step to stand not before her, but alongside her. "Walk with me," he said. "Tell me what happened."

"She's my sister." In a quiet voice, looking up at him with a frightened look. "My only sister."

She identified herself as Ruth Place and said she lived in nearby Beechview. A neighbor had alerted her when the first patrol car arrived. "That son-of-a-bitch has beaten her for years. He doesn't work. He lives off her, then waits for the weekend to batter her. I've tried to tell her—" She stopped, began to weep, then let it all out, her body heaving as she sobbed.

"Take it slow. I'm not going anywhere."

Between gulps for air, she choked out the words, "How is she? Will she be all right?"

"I don't have a report on her condition. As soon as I do—"

"I should go to the hospital."

"I'll take you once you've calmed down. You don't want her to see you like this."

"No," she said, and wiped a sleeve across her nose. "That wouldn't be right."

Novak led her to his own unmarked cruiser and sat beside her. "What did you mean, we told her not to press charges?"

"He did this to her two weekends ago. She called me to pick her up. Wanted to stay at my place. When I got here, two of your officers were waiting. This time, she wanted him in jail. One of them—"

"An officer?"

"Yeah. He started questioning her. Did she really want to do that? Did she know the time she would spend in court? Did she realize what it would do to her husband? He talked her out of it. If he hadn't done that, she wouldn't be headed for the hospital now."

"Chief!"

Novak looked up as Gordon Horvath advanced. Novak's outstretched arm signaled him to leave them alone, but the detective shook his head. Novak arched forward, staring at his officer as he spread both hands, palms down. As Novak continued to stare, Horvath repeated the motion.

Turning back to the woman, Novak said, "Do you recall this officer's name?"

She told him.

"Ms. Place, I'm sorry to have to tell you this..."

———

Novak arrived early at headquarters Monday before the detectives had reported. He checked to make sure the county had processed and charged Frank Matola. Satisfied that the district attorney had the case under control, he reviewed the notes from his conversation with Ruth Place during the early morning hours.

After three-plus decades in law enforcement, he'd seen—if not everything—plenty, and he didn't let much get to him. But the story Ruth Place told kept him awake when he crawled into bed. Even after he'd gone to sleep, he'd been so restless that Barbara had moved into the guest bedroom.

Over coffee and a bagel, he apologized for disturbing her sleep and explained the reason for his disquiet, then dashed to the station. Now he waited, reading a report from two weeks before, examining arrest records, and making notes to himself as he plotted his course of action.

"You wanted to see me, Chief?" Dwayne Foreman was a veteran patrolman, close to retirement, and one of the few men Novak had known before taking over.

Novak sat quietly while Foreman twirled his hat, waiting for whatever was on the chief's mind. "The place smells great," he said. "Norma said you and your wife swabbed it down Saturday."

Novak nodded and got down to business. "Two weeks ago, you responded to a domestic disturbance call on Farmington Avenue, a couple named Matola. Do you recall it?"

"Yes, sir."

"And Deputy McMahon went with you, correct?"

"The girl—Officer Barnwell—was on another call. I needed backup."

"What did you find when you arrived?"

Foreman described the scene. Irene Matola bleeding from a cut on her mouth, sporting red welts on her face and arms that would soon turn to bruises. Her husband sprawled across the sofa, unrepentant. Overturned furniture and a broken lamp around him. Curious neighbors gathered outside the home.

"Did Mrs. Matola make a statement?"

"She told us she and her husband had argued over money or his drinking or something. Maybe both. And he'd hit her. I wrote a report," he said.

"I've read it." Novak lifted the file and tossed it back on the desk. "Something is missing, though. Did Mrs. Matola request that you take any action?"

"No."

"No? She placed the call, didn't she? She must have wanted something from you."

"At first she did, but she changed her mind."

"What caused her to do that?"

Foreman shifted in his chair as though sensing for the first time where this was headed.

"Have you read yesterday's log?"

"Not yet. Norma grabbed me when I came in—"

"She's dead." Novak leaned back, running both hands through his hair. "Frank Matola beat his wife again last night, only this time she suffered a brain hemorrhage. She died in the ambulance en route to UPMC Mercy."

"Jesus!"

"Her sister blames us for her death. She claims Irene wanted to press charges but that we dissuaded her from issuing a PFA against her husband."

Foreman said nothing. Novak waited him out, using silence as a strategy. "McMahon talked her out of it. He—he didn't mean any harm. He says we should do what we can to keep families together."

Novak maintained his silence, waiting for the rest. "He didn't tell her she couldn't file charges. He just explained what she was likely to go through, how she'd have to support herself if he wasn't drawing a salary." Which he wasn't, Novak knew, since he was out of work.

Novak thanked the patrolman, instructing him to remain silent. He sat at his desk, fought a wave of nausea, and considered his next step. Before confronting McMahon, he'd have to make certain this was not just an isolated incident. He knew who might tell him, but this officer was on the evening shift.

After checking personnel records for an address, he told Norma Showalter he had an appointment, leaving before she could question him.

LYDIA BARNWELL TOOK a step back when she saw Novak at her door. He knew the look. *Why has my boss turned up unannounced? Is he after something?*

"Forgive the intrusion," he said. "Something has come up that I hope you can help me with, but I need to keep it in confidence."

"Oh" She stepped aside, inviting him in.

Inexpensive Scandinavian furniture filled her second-floor apartment. Novak pictured her sitting on the floor, a hex driver in hand, attaching lengths of polished aluminum to the underside of white pressboard. His second impression was how neat the apartment looked. From the small row of magazines arrayed on the coffee table to the potted plants centered on four rows of a narrow étagère, everything had its place.

She offered him coffee, but he declined, signaling that he was here on business, not on a social call. "Nice uniform," she said.

"I picked it up Saturday. I'm not comfortable in it, but..." He paused mid-sentence, not wanting to share his thoughts.

"Well, you look official." She motioned him into one of two metal and cloth armchairs and took a seat on the matching sofa. "And thanks for dealing with that mold. I heard you scrubbed it down. You should have called me."

His investigator's eye took in a Pullman kitchen and a hallway to the left that appeared to lead to two bedrooms with a bathroom between them. She followed his gaze and leaned forward, clearing her throat to distract him. *It's habit. I don't know who you're sleeping with and don't care to.*

"I came to you rather than meeting at HQ because I recall how nervous you were about reporting your discovery of Chief Russell's private business."

"You want me to tattle again."

"Domestic disturbances like last night's. How do we handle them?"

She sighed long and hard, her expression bordering on a sneer.

"If you look at our records over the past year or two, which I suspect you have—"

"Yes."

"—you'll see that we make few arrests following domestic A&Bs."

"And that's because…"

"Because we discourage them. It's policy, but unofficial, not in writing. 'Keep families intact. Talk the perpetrator down. Warn the victim of the consequences and complications.'"

To the left, he heard a toilet flush. "It's next door," she said. "These walls are thin."

Which would have been unnecessary to say if the sound had come from an adjoining unit. The next apartment was to the right. There was someone else living here. Novak forged on as though he hadn't noticed. "Whose policy is it?"

She sighed again, ran a hand through her tight curls, and looked away.

"I'm posing the same question to other officers." When she still seemed reluctant, he said, "As you know, Irene Matola is dead. She called us two weeks ago to report her husband. Her sister says we discouraged her from filing a report. She's furious, says she's meeting with an attorney. It may cost the borough a lot of money. But that's not my primary concern."

"It was always there," she said, meeting his gaze. "As long as I've been with the department, there's been this attitude about keeping the lid on. But over the past year, the deputy chief has made it less a suggestion than a rule. I encouraged a woman to bring charges last year. Even helped her file a protective order. McMahon called me on the carpet, said I was exceeding my authority, ordered me not to do it again."

Did you report it? Of course not. To whom would you go? We're too small to have an internal affairs officer. As the only woman on the force…

"I suspect there's a mark on my record."

Novak shook his head. *Do you think he's stupid enough to document it?*

He stood, asked a few more questions, then said, "Thank you for your honesty. I know this puts you in an untenable position, but know that I have your back."

"But how long will you be here?"

"I thought I'd made that clear."

"Chief—" she looked down, seemed to consider, then bored into him with those transfixing eyes. "I know what you said, but something's going on."

"Such as?"

"He hasn't mentioned it to me. He scarcely speaks to me about anything. But he's told others not to get too comfortable with you. That's how he put it to one officer. 'Don't get too used to him. He won't be here long.' Do you have any idea what he means?"

"No," he said, regretting that, after she had been so open with him, he was lying to her.

"HE'S STRUCK AGAIN."

Holding his cell phone to his ear, Novak bolted from bed, fighting a wave of vertigo as he stood. He moved into the hallway to avoid waking Barbara. "Where? How long ago? Anyone hurt?"

"We got the call at 11:10," Lydia Barnwell said. "A convenience store on Cranmore Road and Herschell. The attendant emptied the till and the currency bag. No shots were fired, but Detective Mayfield can't get any more out of her."

"Have you notified County?"

"They're on their way."

"So am I."

It took him five minutes to jump into a pair of jeans, a sweatshirt, and boots. Another eight to reach the store. The flashing strobes of two Boyleston patrol cars illuminated the market. As he entered,

Novak greeted the officers and spotted the attendant, a large woman who appeared to be in her late fifties, with straight salt-and-pepper hair and rolls of fat around her biceps and lower arms. She sat on a stool behind the counter, her elbows resting on the surface, her hands trembling as she clasped a string of rosary beads. Her lips moved, but Novak heard no sound.

He introduced himself. The woman raised her head but didn't speak.

"Are you all right?" he asked.

Her dark eyes darted back and forth. Still, she said nothing.

"She's frightened," Mayfield said. "I can't get her to talk to me."

Novak smiled at the woman. She looked away. He turned and wandered into the parking lot, motioning Barnwell to join him. "Have you tried speaking with her?"

"No, I'm supposed to help secure the exterior."

"Come with me," he said. She followed him into the store and, at his direction, approached the frightened woman.

"Hello," she said. "My name is Lydia Barnwell."

"*Hola.*" The woman smiled and held out her hand. "*Soy Maria Elena Velasquez.*"

"*Cómo estás?*"

"*Estoy bien, pero tengo miedo.*"

Novak whistled under his breath, but Barnwell ignored him.

"*¿Te lastimaste?*"

"*No. Solo estoy asustada. Nunca me ha pasado nada como esto.*"

"*Entiendo. Estás a salvo ahora.*"

Barnwell turned to translate the conversation, but Novak said, "Don't stop. Continue talking with her. Fill me in later."

The woman continued to quake, running through her rosary beads with trembling fingers. Barnwell asked her a question, but she glanced at Novak without speaking.

"She's afraid of you for some reason. Can you—?"

Novak walked away as the county's crime lab arrived. He explained the victim's hesitancy and asked them to hold off for a few minutes. "My officer is bilingual and experienced. She won't let anything contaminate the scene."

They backed off and waited, the victim now eyeing all of them. And Novak got it. He walked toward the two women huddled together at the counter. Barnwell, seeing the fear mount in the woman's eyes, turned as he approached.

"Tell her I don't care that she doesn't have papers. My mother is an immigrant. My only interest is in finding who did this."

Barnwell smiled and translated. Mrs. Velazquez looked up, beaming at him, and said, *"Muchas gracias."*

But I have no idea how County will handle this.

Ten minutes later, Barnwell thanked the woman and led her from the store. County detectives had yet to arrive, so Novak and Barnwell bundled the woman into her car and said goodnight.

"Where did you learn Spanish?"

"Ich spreche auch Deutsch. Parlo un po' italiano."

"Now you're just showing off."

She reared back her head, her blonde curls ruffling in the night breeze, and laughed. "My father's retired Air Force. Wherever he was stationed, I picked up the local language. I even speak Texan."

Novak recalled her nailing the origin of the Shiner Bock logo. "It's a useful skill; if we ever need Slovak, I can help. So what do we know?"

Barnwell recounted what she'd learned. The woman was from Honduras. She had journeyed northward two years before, after a gang had raped and murdered her daughter. Her nephew, who ran the store for a man she didn't know, was a legal resident. Because he was suffering from a cold and fever, she had taken his place behind the counter that night so he wouldn't lose his job.

The robber had entered the store at closing time and said something in English the woman hadn't understood. When she answered in Spanish, he'd responded in kind, promising not to hurt her if she handed over the money. When she did so, he'd left the store on foot. She had no idea where he'd gone and hadn't noticed a vehicle.

"She was terrified," Barnwell said. "Coming from Honduras, she's seen it all, so she hid beneath the counter until another customer entered and found her. He called it in. For obvious reasons, she didn't want to involve us and didn't know what else to do."

"She must have called her nephew."

"She said she was too frightened to do anything."

Her description of the man matched the others they had received, but the county would need to retrieve the surveillance images and make certain they matched.

"She told me something that may be significant," Barnwell said. "He's not only Hispanic, he's a fellow countryman, *un hondureño*."

"How can she be certain?"

"He used Honduran slang. She's fairly certain he's from San Pedro Sula."

Novak blew out a lungful of air. At long last, progress.

"What will happen to her?" Barnwell said.

"I don't know, but I'll do what I can to keep ACPD from notifying the Feds."

———

THE OFFICE, usually bustling at this hour, was quiet when Novak arrived the following morning, ready to confront McMahon over his handling of Irene Matola's complaint two weeks before.

It was not to be. Mayfield caught his eye, nodded toward his office door, and whispered, "Trouble."

Trouble took the form of Council President Doug Lentz, who sat in one of his guest chairs, hat in his hand, foot tapping. "Isn't it rather late?"

"I've been working since 7:30," Novak said. He hung up his jacket and sat down at his desk, hands folded in front of him.

"We need to talk," Lentz said.

Novak inverted his right hand, extending an invitation, but said not a word.

"There was another armed robbery last night," the councilman said.

"Yes, I was on the scene."

"The chairwoman of the business alliance called me this morning. She's concerned."

"As am I. As are we all."

"She feels we're not doing enough to bring this creep to justice."

"And what did you tell her?"

Lentz sat erect in his chair. "Don't try putting me on the defensive."

Novak put both hands to his chest, the picture of innocence. "You came to relay a complaint from a prominent citizen. I'm trying to learn what she said."

He leaned back. "I told her I'd find out."

"Did you tell her half our patrol officers and all three detectives are working on this? That we've circulated his name and description to every business? That we've interviewed the manager of every—"

"There's some feeling that we're not pursuing this correctly, that we've gone off on a tangent."

"Whose feeling? What tangent?"

"You're giving too much weight to the possibility that this suspect works for a restaurant, and you're not pursuing more promising avenues," he said, ignoring Novak's first question.

"We're pursuing every avenue. The council gets a daily email from me, detailing the steps we're taking. The plastic gloves are a clue, but only one. The suspect's use of a motorbike is another. And thanks to the talents of one of my officers, we now suspect the perpetrator is not Asian, as we first thought, but a Honduran immigrant. We even know what part of Honduras he's from. The investigating officer from Allegheny County PD is delighted with the progress we're making. That's where I've been this morning."

"I'm sorry, Novak. I don't mean to seem accusatory. It's just—she called me, and I have to ask the right questions."

"I appreciate that."

Lentz rose to leave, then turned at the office door. "Just one more thing. These robberies have to be our top priority right now."

"Of course."

"We don't have the luxury of spending time on side issues."

"Such as?"

"Past cases that were closed long ago."

Novak ushered the council president to the door leading to the administrative wing. "My challenge," he said in a voice barely above a whisper, "is a subordinate officer who questions every decision we make in this case and never responds to emergencies. I was called to the scene last night because the first responders couldn't reach their superior. Rather than working on this case, which I agree is our top priority, he spends his time spreading rumors and creating discord."

Lentz turned to face him. "Who is this officer?"

"I'm the chief," Novak said, "and I'll deal with it. It's not the only matter before me right now. I'd handle them all if I could spare time from these robberies. As you said, that's the priority."

CHAPTER SEVEN
MAYBE THIS ISN'T OVER

"Do you have a minute?" Calvin Mayfield stood in his doorway, a marker in his right hand.

Novak motioned him in, but Mayfield said, "No, you should see this."

He followed the detective to his desk, on which he'd spread a map of the South Hills.

"I know Horvath is in charge of the investigation—"

Novak waved the pending apology aside. "We're all in this. Go ahead."

"Last night's robbery broke a pattern."

"You noticed that, too. All the rest have been on Saturdays."

"He's desperate," Mayfield said. "When he murdered Adi Patel last week, he didn't get away with a penny. He struck last night because he needed money."

"Strengthening the theory that he's an addict. What else?"

"He operates only on Pittsburgh's South Side and three adjoining boroughs. Right in here."

Novak leaned forward, studying the area Mayfield had outlined on the map.

"At first, we thought our man had it in for Indian immigrants, but he hit a Honduran this weekend and two brothers and two White guys in neighboring jurisdictions in the past. The only reason he robbed these Indian immigrants is that they own the markets in Boyleston."

Novak rubbed his hands together. "We inferred a causal relationship."

"But this doesn't mean none exists. All these shops serve prepared food. Cold sandwiches, burgers, burritos that you heat in a microwave. Packaged slices of pie, fruit cups...meals on the go."

"And I presume they're all served by the same company," Novak said.

"You got it. Norton Food Services located in Carnegie. It delivers to these twenty shops, all on the same route."

Novak peered at the map as Mayfield explained. He'd marked the eight markets the holdup man had hit in red, using blue for the twelve that he had not. He drew a green ring that encompassed the locations marked in red, then pointed to a single blue dot within it. "This is where he'll hit next."

Novak scratched his neck, twisting his mouth to one side. "I see the logic, but let's ask Norton who drives that route."

"I already have. His name is Rufus Boyer. He's never been out of the country and doesn't know anyone from Central America. He has been with the company for years, and Norton's manager says he's a model employee. Boyer has no clue why someone would do this to his customers."

"And Norton—?"

"—Has no one from Central America working there."

"Are we sure this isn't the only company—"

"Three others serve Allegheny County. Each supplies packaged food to South Hills markets, but none have been robbed recently. These holdups have something to do with the Norton Food Services truck that runs this specific route."

"So we know there's a pattern," Novak said, "but we can't

connect it to a suspect. Our best course is to stake out this store on Saturday night. Nice work, Detective. I'll alert the ACPD."

NOVAK RETURNED HOME FOR LUNCH, but after staring into the refrigerator for a half-minute decided he couldn't eat. Lentz's challenge, an implicit acceptance of the poison McMahon was spreading, was disheartening. Novak was giving his all to this job, trying to reform a broken department while dealing with the most serious crime spree it had faced in years.

Removing his uniform, he lay on the comforter, staring at the ceiling. As the room spun, he turned onto his side, focusing on his father's portrait on the wall to arrest the motion. Then he struggled into the bathroom and wretched until nothing more came up.

He should have called in sick but couldn't. He faced two issues with which he must deal—the handling of domestic violence victims before anyone else got hurt, and McMahon's treachery.

There were only three reasons his deputy—*my "deputy!"*—was spreading word that Novak was a short-timer. The most straightforward was that McMahon was competing for departmental loyalty. *Follow me, not him.* The second was that someone—Mayor Tifton or Councilor Frain—was using McMahon to undermine him.

The third reason was one Novak didn't want to consider: that McMahon knew why he had left the Pittsburgh Police Bureau. If that were the case, he probably was working with Tifton to spring it on the council at an opportune moment.

Perhaps Barbara was right. He should have addressed the issue at the start and let events take their course. It was still an option. He needed to be sure how much the man had discovered and whom he had told.

He arose, dressed, ate a few saltines, and returned to the station.

"Marvin Ross is looking for you, says it's urgent. I tried reaching you by radio, but—"

"Thanks, Norma. I'll find him."

He entered the administrative wing, tapped on Ross' door, and entered without waiting for permission. The city attorney was on the phone and motioned him into a chair. "The chief just entered. I'll get back to you."

"The Matola murder," Novak said without waiting to be asked.

"All hell's breaking loose. The victim's sister has hired an attorney and is threatening a lawsuit. She claims your officers—"

"I know what she says. I intended to deal with it this morning, but I was sidetracked." He unrolled everything that had happened over the past few days and told the attorney what he'd learned.

"I haven't confronted McMahon. I need to confirm the facts with two other officers. If I don't get the story from multiple sources, I'll leave one of my best people open to retaliation."

"Half an hour?" Ross said. "Then get him in here."

Novak returned to the police wing, summoning Officer Kimrey and Detective Mayfield, both of whom he felt he could trust. They backed up what Barnwell and Foreman had told him about how McMahon handled domestic assaults.

The deputy chief had signed himself out for lunch and wasn't responding to the dispatcher's messages. Novak had Norma Showalter call his cell and order him to return to HQ immediately. Noting that the deputy's car was parked in the lot, he opened his computer to view the security camera covering the front of the building. He watched as McMahon emerged a few minutes later from Mayor Tifton's Buick.

Novak met him as he sauntered into the bullpen. "Follow me," he said. He led them into the administrative wing, past the office of the mayor, who looked at them with unrestrained curiosity, and tapped on the door of the city attorney. Novak motioned McMahon into an office chair and pulled his own alongside Ross' desk, very much the man in charge.

McMahon looked from one to the other, his characteristic arrogance absent.

"Two weeks ago, I asked you what we were working on. You told me," and here Novak flipped to the first page in his notebook and read aloud, "'One guy over on Farmington beat up his wife pretty good, but she won't press charges.' What did you mean, 'she won't press charges?'"

McMahon shifted his weight in the chair, leaning forward as though attempting to minimize his height. "Just that she declined to press charges."

"After you suggested she not do so," Novak said.

"I—I didn't tell her not to."

"What did you say?"

"Is this an interrogation?"

Novak and the attorney glanced at each other, then nodded. "Yes. As I'm sure you know, Frank Matola beat his wife to death this weekend."

McMahon remained stone-faced.

Ross picked up the thread. "Her sister is threatening legal action. We need to go back to the night of April 20th, hear what she asked and your response and compare them to the other statements we've taken."

"I followed procedure."

"Which procedure?" Novak said.

"We're to keep families together whenever we can."

"I've read every departmental policy at least twice. I recall nothing like that."

"How *would* you remember?" McMahon said.

So there it was. Out in the open. His "deputy" had been probing his past and had uncovered his secret—at least part of it. Novak smiled, forcing himself to remain calm.

"If you can cite the policy, please do," he said.

"It has been our policy since long before you got here."

"If it is not in the policy handbook, it's not policy," Ross said. "If you talked her out of filing a complaint, we could be liable."

McMahon nodded. "Okay, I'll make sure the men know they're to remain neutral."

"No...and no. We're not just to remain neutral. We are to support the victim. And *you* won't convey that; I will. You're suspended with pay at least until we determine whether Mrs. Place sues."

Under the attorney's supervision, Novak took the man's badge, identification, vehicle keys, and sidearm. McMahon showed no emotion during all this, but as he left the office, he glanced over his shoulder with a smug look that suggested he expected to have the last laugh.

Novak motioned Calvin into his office. After revealing his decision to suspend McMahon, he said, "I need the support of a senior officer who's smart, competent, and trustworthy. That narrows the field considerably. I'm appointing you acting deputy chief. What do you say?"

"I'll do whatever you need, but I've never supervised anyone before."

"Tomorrow, you won't be able to say that."

He called every member of the council, taking them through what had happened. He began with Bernie Jackson, outlining to the veteran council member how he intended to operate in McMahon's absence, a plan Jackson endorsed. He suggested that Novak report on departmental issues at a closed council session the following week. Novak added that to his script as he continued his calls.

Only one councilman registered any objection, and it came from a predictable source. "McMahon's a good man. He's run the department single-handedly for months, perhaps longer," Byron Frain said.

"As I explained, he failed to follow department policy, even ordering officers to circumvent it. His actions contributed to a woman's death, her family is threatening to sue, and he misled us when we interviewed him."

"That's not how he tells it."

It did not surprise Novak that the suspended officer had been working the phones. "Speak with the city attorney. He was present for the full interview. I acted under Mr. Ross' guidance."

Novak did not mention the other incidents over the past two weeks, since anything he told Frain would find its way back to McMahon. He'd hold his fire until the council meeting.

At the change in shift, Novak called everyone together to outline the plan. By then, he suspected, none of this was news, but he went over it anyway, operating by the book. Only Detective Horvath had questions, and from their content, he assumed McMahon had already shared his version of events. The man would not go away quietly.

He spent another hour with Mayfield, outlining the division of duties. Novak would supervise the other two detectives while Mayfield managed the patrol division. As the only Black officer in the department, he would encounter enough resistance without having to oversee two men senior to him.

They discussed the status of personnel and shifts and reviewed every outstanding case facing the department. With a plan in place for trapping the armed robber, they would suspend the house-to-house search. Novak offered to shift other cases Mayfield had been handling, but he declined. "I'll pull some extra hours, and if I see it's too much, I'll let you know."

They sealed the partnership with a handshake. Pausing at the door, Mayfield said, "There's one thing. Do I have to wear a uniform?"

Novak chuckled. "I'm afraid so. It happens to the best of us."

He spent the rest of the afternoon compiling a comprehensive report on what he'd found during his first two weeks on the job. He wouldn't read it to the council verbatim, but he wanted to come prepared for any challenge.

"I hate it," he told Barbara after dinner. "Not the policing, but the politics, the personalities, the administrivia."

꙳ Ha ha!

"Nothing you did today was trivial," she said. "Each day, you're making this a better police force. It's your job."

"And I hate it. I feel like I'm on a treadmill, and it's going faster than I can."

Besides the armed robbery, he had two investigations to pursue, and another day had slipped by without his making progress on them.

———————

NOVAK AND MAYFIELD sat on upturned milk containers, sweating as the heat built up in the cramped corners of the storage room of the convenience store. It was warm for a May evening, and the air conditioner was so noisy they had shut it off.

A county detective manned the counter, a Smith & Wesson .38 loaded and within easy reach just below it. All three men inside wore Kevlar vests. The ACPD had stationed two unmarked vehicles to the east and west of the store on Versailles Avenue, and two cruisers lay in wait a quarter mile in either direction. Across the street, two patrol officers watched the market from a closed and darkened auto supply store.

All units could monitor conversations at the counter, as hidden microphones transmitted every sound. A crew had arrived in the predawn hours to install electronic surveillance, including two lipstick cameras that were trained on the counter. The surveillance team had been in place since eight o'clock. The store was one of the few in town licensed to sell beer, creating a steady parade of customers. Many were teenagers, whom the "proprietor" turned away, but Novak made a note to stake the place out during future weekends.

Three hours elapsed. It was now closing time, the moment when the robber normally made his move. Novak had risked his reputation with the county, and as the minutes ticked by, he tried to remain optimistic. What if they'd picked the wrong market? What if the killer had taken this Saturday night off or gone to ground after revealing himself to his fellow countryman the week before? What if Mayfield had it all wrong—seeing a pattern where none existed?

Struggling to remember the points Mayfield had made leading to the night, Novak damned his spotty memory. He'd written everything down and had been over his notes at least three times. Each time he'd reviewed it, the reasoning had seemed solid.

"I hope I got this right," Mayfield said in a low voice.

"Relax." Novak concealed his own reservations. "We built it, and he will come."

"Subject matching the description approaching the intersection from the east," a voice said over the radio.

"Unit Three," a watcher from the auto supply store said. "We have him in sight. He's paused at the edge of the parking lot. Wearing jeans, a black and yellow jacket, and a Pirates baseball cap."

It sounded all wrong. "What color are his shoes?" Novak whispered into his shoulder-mounted microphone.

"Can't tell. He's reaching into his pocket for something. Wait. He turned, he's looking the other way..."

Novak held his breath as the subject examined his surroundings. Not a sound from Mayfield, who was doing the same.

"He turned again," said the disembodied voice. "He's approaching the entrance."

Novak and Mayfield heard a chime as the door opened, but from their vantage point, they couldn't see who had entered. They waited for him to approach the counter, but nothing happened.

"What's the status?" the voice on the radio demanded.

"He's at the cooler in the back," the officer at the counter whispered. "Looking for something. Can't see him. Wait—approaching now."

The radio crackled. "All units move in."

Novak and Mayfield remained poised behind the door like coiled springs. Novak saw the man's back as he passed by. He looked down at his shoes. Gray. Dull gray. Had he—

The subject slammed two six-packs onto the counter and reached into his jacket pocket. "And a pack of Camels," he said, which emerged as "Anapagakemmels."

The officer behind the counter later said he could smell alcohol on the man's breath as he observed his clumsy effort to extract his wallet.

"I'm sorry, but I can't sell alcohol to you," he said. "You'll have to leave."

"Whazzamadder?"

"You've had enough to drink. I can't sell to you. Leave. Now."

The unmarked cars tore into the lot, followed seconds later by the patrol cars. Novak and Mayfield stepped from their hiding places.

"G'dam Moslem," the drunk said.

"Crap," Novak said. "I've got to pee." He made for the men's room.

Only hours later, when they'd examined the surveillance videos overhanging the gas pumps, did they spot the image of a figure on a motorbike as it turned out of a side street a block away and raced west on Versailles.

———

"I MET WITH BRIDEY YESTERDAY AFTERNOON," Mariel said. Sunday dinner was over, Novak had cleared the dishes as the women visited, Izabela had gone upstairs for her afternoon nap, and Mariel had parked Jennifer in front of her iPad in the family room. Now she relaxed, a cup of coffee before her, as she related the conversation to her parents.

"And?" Barbara said.

"I took Jen with me to keep Amy occupied while we talked, but I didn't fool her. On the way out the door, she said, 'You're going to talk to Mrs. O'Connor about the murder, aren't you?' I couldn't lie to her. I pledged her to silence."

"Bridey," Novak said. "Will she let us speak to Amy?"

Mariel was not to be deflected from telling her story her way.

"Bridey works at the bakery on Saturdays, so I timed it to a quarter past three, right after they close. She was in her uniform when we got there. She said she needed to change."

"Mariel, please."

"Just let her finish, Karol."

Novak sighed, unable to hide his impatience.

"Amy came running down the stairs, squealing with delight as soon as she saw Jen. And your granddaughter was a trooper. She invited her to play outside—it's really been warm, hasn't it? But Amy suggested they play in her room."

Mariel told how she waited as Bridey went upstairs, returning in a pair of gray slacks and a well-worn pink cotton top.

"What kind of shoes was she wearing?"

"White loafers. What difference does it make, Dad?"

"Karol, stop it."

Their daughter shrugged. "She immediately asked me what was wrong. I'd wanted to ease her into the conversation, but she got right to the point."

Unlike my daughter.

"'Has Amy done something at school?'

"'No, nothing like that,' I said. She sprawled into a stuffed chair, both arms on the rests as though ready to spring at a moment's notice.

"I said, 'My Dad, Chief Novak, has been looking into the murder of your mother.'

"'I don't want to talk about it.' She snapped at me, just like that.

"I told her you haven't found anything, but that you'd like to meet with the two of them to reassure Amy that the investigation was handled properly. And maybe ask her a few questions. She got really nervous. She said, 'About what?' Her body was so rigid, I thought she was about to attack me.

"I told her you wonder what aroused Amy's curiosity—whether someone is taunting her at school. It was the best I could come up with. And she said, 'If she gets bullied, I'll handle it.'"

Mariel looked from her father to her mother and back again.

"She said—and I recall her exact words—'I have lived with this my entire life. I discovered my mother's body. I had to alert the neighbors. I had to sit in a county facility for hours until they got in touch with my grandma. Sitting there alone, terrified, remembering what my mother looked like, lying in bed with a bag tied over her head.'

"She leaned forward, her hands were clenched, her eyes drilled right through me. 'And then my father's arrest. Waiting all that time for someone—anyone—to fix things. Having to change schools, enduring jeers when other kids found out, listening to my grandmother mourning my mother and cursing my father—day after day, year after year. It was horrible.'

"So I said, 'Because you suspected he was innocent?'

"And she snarled—pardon my French, but this is what she said—'Because I *know* the son-of-a-bitch is guilty.'"

As THEY LAY in bed later, Novak described the busted stake-out to Barbara. "He knows we're on to him. He's been careless, foolhardy, almost as if he wants to be caught. But now he'll be cautious. We'll have a job taking him down."

"You didn't tell me what you were doing last night," Barbara said.

"I said we hoped to make an arrest."

"Karol, you were in danger. He could have shot you."

"The officer behind the counter was the one at risk. I was hiding. And holding my bladder." He chuckled to himself, but she didn't join in.

"How did your men take McMahon's suspension?" Barbara said.

"There's a woman, too. Don't forget that." She didn't react to his gentle needling. "I sensed some relief, but I could be imagining it. Or it could be they're aware of the tension between us and are happy not to be caught in the middle anymore."

"And you're certain he knows something."

"He was pointed about it. 'How *would* you remember?' Ross couldn't have missed that."

"I'm sorry. I know you didn't want it to get out."

"Didn't I? I don't recall."

Barbara ignored him. "And Bridey's reaction. I guess that settles it. I was so hoping..."

"I know. But Walsh confessed, and a jury of his peers found him guilty. He's ineligible for a pardon, but the governor has reviewed the case for clemency and turned him down. It's not like I'm looking for something to keep me off the streets."

As he struggled to fall asleep, his thoughts were not on the armed robberies or on McMahon, but on Thomas Walsh. How had his granddaughter learned about the case? What had led her to make that astonishing appeal on his behalf, her birthday wish?

At that moment, a fragment of memory that had been chasing him for days caught up. A name. "Matthew Harris," he said.

"What?" Barbara, half asleep, rolled over and blinked as he turned on the bedside lamp.

"Matthew Harris." He grabbed his ever-present notepad from the nightstand and scrawled the name.

"Maybe this isn't over. I wonder—"

LYDIA BARNWELL

CHAPTER EIGHT
A SLOPPY INVESTIGATION

"Matthew Harris." At a diner on Pittsburgh's South Side, Novak met with Jack Fisher, a veteran captain from the Allegheny PD.

Fisher shook a drop of ketchup off his finger, put down his burger, and wiped his hands on a napkin. "Why dredge up that old name?"

"He was the lead investigator on a murder case in Boyleston back in the late 80s." Fisher raised his gray, bushy eyebrows, the only hair remaining north of his nose.

"Rebecca Walsh," Novak added in response to the unanswered question.

Fisher grunted. "Open and shut, as I recall."

"That's what I thought until Harris' name popped up." He inverted his hands, inviting the older officer to spill.

"Bad cop," Fisher said. "When drugs moved out to the burbs, we transferred him to narcotics. Defendants kept accusing him of planting evidence during traffic stops. They always say that, but these stories were consistent. When the DA looked into it, he also noticed Harris' frequent use of the same jailhouse snitches. His investigators set up a sting, and Harris and his partner fell into it."

He massaged his forehead with his fingertips while Novak

scrawled notes. "It was a shitstorm. Convictions overturned. The guilty walked along with the innocent. The county paid thousands in restitution."

"I remember the case," Novak said. "I didn't recall Harris was the detective."

"How could you forget?"

Novak stared at his now-empty plate.

"You were with the city then, so it didn't affect you. We weren't so lucky."

Fisher wolfed down the rest of the burger, chasing it with a handful of fries. He was right. Harris was a name he *should* have remembered. There were many things he should remember.

Tony Grico hadn't forgotten. Novak recalled the retired detective's look of contempt as he described the investigation. He had misinterpreted his reaction. Grico wasn't reacting to Walsh, but to Matt Harris. Why hadn't he mentioned Harris' dishonorable record during their discussion? Did he assume Novak knew? Or did the blue wall of silence extend over years and decades?

"Are you reopening the Walsh murder?" Fisher asked.

"I didn't intend to, but I should review the file."

"Be my guest. I don't think you'll find anything." Lowering his voice, he said, "I hope to hell you won't."

———

MAYFIELD KNOCKED at his door even though it was open. "You need to take this call, Chief."

"Who is it?"

"Her name is Cecilia Aldershaw. She has a complaint and won't speak to anyone but you. I tried to handle it myself, but since I'm only *acting* deputy chief..."

Novak got the implication. He introduced himself and listened as she complained that she had spent a half-hour trying to get someone to pay attention to her. He knew this wasn't true, since he'd been meeting with all the officers not ten minutes before. Mayfield remained in the doorway, a slight smile on his lips.

"How can I help you?" he said.

"I live in Forest Heights," she said. From her tone, Novak had already worked that out. "At least three days a week, I take Belmont Road into town. There's a sharp turn just past Margate Restaurant."

Novak knew the spot. Belmont Road twisted and turned as it wound its way down the side of a hill into Pittsburgh.

"There's a deer crossing sign in the middle of the turn," she said. "I want you to move it."

"Mrs. Aldershaw, we can't do that. It's in place to warn drivers like yourself that deer frequently cross the road there."

Novak looked up to see Sergeant Mayfield covering his mouth with one hand while wrapping the other around his middle.

"And they've nearly run into me on several occasions," she said. "The most recent time was last night. A whole herd of them came running out of nowhere, down the hill and across the road right in front of me."

"I know. It's nearly happened to me."

"That's why I want you to move the sign. It's hazardous in the middle of the curve."

"Mrs. Aldershaw, why would we move it? It's there for a purpose."

Mayfield was now doubled over, and Officer Kimrey stood behind him, grinning like a schoolboy who'd just found a Playboy centerfold.

The caller nearly screamed at him. "Move it somewhere else, of course—somewhere safer for the deer to cross, somewhere you can see them coming."

Novak leaned forward, his hand against his forehead, stifling laughter.

"I see," he said. "But here's the thing. We don't handle road signs. City council is in charge of that."

Mayfield laughed so loudly that Novak covered the mouthpiece. Kimrey turned and motioned other officers to join them.

"Who would I talk to over there?"

"I would start with Mayor Tifton. His number is 412-721..."

She had him repeat the number.

"And if he's busy, Councilman Frain chairs the budget committee." He read out the number, which she repeated. She thanked him. Novak disconnected the call, but continued speaking.

"Another thing they may want to consider is installing a crosswalk and pedestrian signal at that spot. When the deer want to cross, they can push the button with their forehooves..."

Mayfield laughed so hard he slid down the doorjamb and landed on his ass.

DURING HIS FIRST week as chief, Novak had noticed gaps in McMahon's employment and was struck by his vagueness in discussing his background. He called the police department at Norwalk State University, asked to speak with the chief, and identified himself, explaining that he was new to the job. "One of our officers was on your force for three years. He recently applied for promotion. I'm researching his experience and expertise."

"What's this officer's name?" Chief Frank Barnett said.

"Daryl McMahon."

"McMahon. Yes, I remember him. What do you need to know?"

Barnett explained that, far from just being "campus cops," the NSU police force was a municipal law enforcement agency, responsible for security and criminal investigations at the university and empowered to make arrests. McMahon had served as a patrol officer for two years, then had been promoted to investigator.

"According to our records, he left in 2013," Novak said. "Does that sound right?"

"Yes, in November of that year."

"Why did he leave?"

"He had a job offer from another police force."

"Do you recall which one?"

"No, not offhand. Since he was no longer on the force, where he worked next didn't concern us."

"He left in November, but he didn't start his next job until the following May. That's six months."

"I wouldn't know about that," Barnett said.

"But you say he left to take another job. Six months is quite a gap, wouldn't you say?"

"I can't speak to that. You'd have to ask him."

"Did he leave on good terms?"

Barnett's hesitation was long enough to drive a truck through. "He quit, if that's what you mean."

"He wasn't terminated?"

"No."

"Would you recommend him for promotion in a police force of about a dozen?"

"That depends. From what to what?"

"To a top administrative post?"

"Like chief? You're the chief."

"To assistant chief."

"It's been a long time since we worked together. He works for you now, so you know him better than I."

"Chief Barnett, did he leave the university in good standing?" The same question posed differently.

"He resigned, as I said. I can't discuss personnel matters. Why don't you speak with Human Resources? I'd be happy to transfer you."

Novak sensed he would get no further and permitted himself to be handed off. He was soon engaged in a similar conversation with an officious HR officer whose job was to prevent any information about employees, past or present, escaping from the university's electronic file cabinets.

"We cannot share information on former personnel," she said.

"Did he leave under favorable circumstances?"

"He resigned. That's all I'm allowed to tell you."

"Is he eligible for re-employment?"

"I'm not permitted to divulge any other information."

Further communication seemed pointless, but it had taken him nearly twenty minutes to get this far into the labyrinth of the university's bureaucracy. Since they'd taken so much of his time, he felt duty-bound to take more of theirs.

"As I said, I'm chief of police of a Pittsburgh suburb. Let us suppose, for the sake of argument, that I inquired about a former university employee who was being considered for a position of great fiscal responsibility. Let us also suppose that the university had allowed this individual to resign after he had misappropriated tens of thousands of dollars from student athletic funds." Novak marshaled every bit of bureaucratic jargon known to him.

"Let us further suppose that you refused to divulge that information, Ms. Anderson, that we hired this individual, and that he misappropriated low-income housing funds, forcing the borough to turn poor residents into the streets in the middle of winter. Do you *suppose*," he said, raising his voice, "we would hesitate to sue the hell out of your benighted institution for withholding this vital information?"

"Good day, sir."

Novak regarded his dead handset with grim satisfaction. He might have drilled a dry hole, but there was oil somewhere in this field. He considered calling the powers-that-be in Doubleday, Ohio, but refrained. It was a small town, and he suspected McMahon would learn of his call within minutes.

Like a good attorney, he would ask no more questions until he knew the answers.

THE SEVEN-MEMBER COUNCIL met on the second and fourth Thursdays of each month in a room that held seats for thirty citizens. Civic groups had asked the council to expand its chambers "to facilitate greater public input," but if there was one thing the members didn't want, it was more kvetching.

That night, citizens filled every seat in the chamber, with fifteen more standing at the back.

Council President Lentz gaveled the meeting to order and recognized Mayor Tifton to update recent construction projects. Lentz made a series of public announcements, chief among them changes to the route of the Memorial Day parade the following Monday. He recognized three high school students who'd worked in various city departments over the past semester.

Novak expected that most of the public comments would concern how his department was handling the armed robbery investigation, but only Brenda Newell, the chairwoman of the Business Alliance, had come to address it. She spoke in measured tones, expressing the concern of the business community. Novak recounted the steps the department was taking to support what, he reminded her, was a county investigation. "These robberies are our top priority. We have devoted more man-hours to this case than to any other in a decade."

Seemingly satisfied, she thanked him and left the meeting.

Almost everyone else was there to demand that the borough install a traffic light at the entrance to a townhome community off Brinker Road. Lentz asked for one representative of the homeowners association to represent the group, setting up yowls of protest from others who wished for their five minutes of glory. Relenting, Lentz allowed four more citizens to speak.

Half an hour later, Mayor Tifton explained that since Brinker Road was a state highway, the Pennsylvania Department of Transportation must approve any changes in traffic patterns. This required a study which could only be conducted by PennDOT, but the agency refused to fund it. Nothing would happen. No one asked Novak what he thought, which was just as well since he would have said that someone would have to die at this dangerous intersection before the state acted.

The council accepted an easement for a sanitary sewer running beneath private property, approved the purchase of a forklift, and authorized two yield signs at other intersections before adjourning the public meeting and going into a closed session.

With the room cleared, Lentz gaveled the meeting back to order and called on Novak for his report. He took them through the events of the past month, the steps he had taken to support the county's investigation, and the botched stake-out over the previous weekend. On the plus side, Novak said, they had produced new information on the gunman's identity.

Councilwoman Annie Lunate asked for specifics. "We now know he is Hispanic," he said. "Thanks to Officer Lydia Barnwell's language skills, we uncovered some vital new information, but county investigators have asked me to withhold it. They don't want the perpetrator to know how much we've learned about him."

A long sigh and shake of her head showed her disappointment. Everyone wanted to be in the know. With no additional questions, he moved on.

On Barbara's advice, Novak focused on the issue that had led to McMahon's suspension, omitting his insolence and insubordination. After reviewing details of Mrs. Matola's beating and subsequent death, he recounted the confrontation with her sister.

Councilwoman Lunate scowled and heaved another sigh.

As Novak described his decision to probe deeper and his questioning of fellow officers, Councilman Frain studied the ceiling and drummed the eraser end of a pencil on the council table.

Novak nodded toward the city attorney. "When we questioned Deputy McMahon, he insisted that he had followed policy in dealing both with Mrs. Matola's earlier attack and those against other women. There is no such policy. We learned he had disciplined officers who offered assistance to other victims. Our decision to suspend him was not based on just one incident, but on a pattern of behavior he refused to acknowledge."

Aside from the audible reactions of Councilwoman Lunate, the others listened without comment. As Novak concluded, Frain said, "Daryl McMahon is a valued member of this department. He held it together for many months with no expectation of reward. You could have handled this more professionally."

Novak returned his gaze without responding, hoping Ross would come to his defense, but Frain wasn't finished. "You should have told him what you expected and allowed him to continue in his job. Instead, you let personal animosity cloud your judgment."

"I have no animosity toward Officer McMahon," Novak said, fighting to keep his voice level. "It's the other way around. He has opposed every decision I've made since assuming command. He ridicules other officers during meetings. He resists my effort to reestablish a chain of command. I've counseled him on his behavior and done everything possible to conceal our disagreements from others. His attitude remains unchanged. But all this has nothing to do with his suspension."

"We didn't have a choice," Ross said. "McMahon's procedures endanger every victim of domestic violence. Not only does he fail to acknowledge it, his responses border on insubordination. If we go to court, we must show that we dealt with this issue as soon as we became aware of it."

"I'm on the record," Frain said. "You didn't handle this well."

Novak suppressed an urge to shrug.

"There's another issue," Tifton said. "We've had reports that you are delving into an old criminal case that was resolved years ago."

"Which case is that?"

"I won't get into specifics, but others feel you're distracted by matters that are no longer this department's concern."

"I reject that," Novak said. "What others? Where are you getting your information?"

"That's not the issue," Frain said. "As we heard tonight, these robberies have terrified business owners. No one wants to move his business here. It's hurting our economy. And while a killer is at large, our police force is sent off on a fool's errand."

"We are pursuing every lead—"

"Do your duty!" Tifton rose half out of his seat, an accusatory finger leveled at Novak.

"Enough!" Bernie Jackson was on his feet. "You don't know what you're talking about. You have no role here. Chief Novak reports to the council."

"And he's doing a poor job," Frain retorted.

"Quite the contrary." Jackson brandished a typewritten sheet in a shaking hand. "I received this letter today from Albert Starr, Chief of the Allegheny County Police Department. 'Dear Councilman Jackson,'" he read,

> I want to express to you how pleased I am at the changes Chief Novak has made to the Boyleston Police Department.
>
> In the past, I expressed concern at the lack of interagency coordination between your agency and others. This lack of cooperation impeded many criminal investigations. Our efforts to resolve these issues with your previous chief were ignored.
>
> By contrast, Chief Novak has provided exemplary assistance in our current effort to identify and arrest the perpetrator of the South Hills convenience store robberies. The chief and his team have uncovered important clues to aid us in our investigation.
>
> Again, I congratulate you on your excellent choice of leadership.

"I move that this letter be entered into the record and that the council reaffirm its trust in Karol Novak," Jackson said.

Councilwoman Lunate offered a second.

"Discussion? All in favor..." Lentz lowered his gavel.

Novak sat quietly after the adjournment, stunned at the viciousness of the attack.

"Thank you," he said, as Jackson passed before him, adding in a quiet voice, "How did you get that letter?"

Jackson looked from side-to-side, then leaned down. "I wrote it and asked him to sign it. Pretty good, don't you think?"

———————

"THEY AMBUSHED YOU," Barbara said. "Why?"

"Frain's pissed over getting a traffic ticket. Tifton's irate over his loss of authority. McMahon was their pipeline into the department."

"But attacking you like that. Aren't they overreacting?"

Novak had been up half the night puzzling over the same thing. While he was angry, he felt oddly reassured. "The enemies are out in the open now, rather than skulking around. Everyone's seen them at work. If they come at me again, they'll have a tough time."

McMahon to Tifton to Frain. He had broken up their party. Now he could run the department unencumbered.

He checked out early Friday afternoon and headed to the ACPD, located a few miles away in a forbidding brick-and-glass structure next to an abandoned shopping center in Greentree. He stopped by Chief Starr's office to thank him for signing Bernie Jackson's letter and moved on to the criminal division for an update on the Patel probe.

Detective Sergeant Glen Carpenter told him they were working with US Citizenship and Immigration Services to track down every Honduran immigrant known to be living anywhere in the region.

"But he may be here illegally, which means they won't have a line on him." Carpenter assured him they were concealing the identity of Maria Elena Velasquez. While Pittsburgh was not a sanctuary city, it was a city of immigrants, and neither Carpenter nor Chief Starr were inclined to further victimize a refugee.

His official business done, Novak headed to the records department. It took the clerk twenty minutes to find the files in the Rebecca Walsh murder. Novak realized with a pang of guilt that he now thought of it as the Thomas Walsh case, as though he were the victim. The records occupied four vertical boxes, each containing half a ream of paper. Novak had expected more.

He began with the report of Andrew Millar, the first detective on the scene. It picked up where Grico's had left off, describing Millar's effort to secure the crime scene and his initial examination of the bedroom. His description differed from Grico's in two ways. When Millar examined the body, he discovered a torn gap in the plastic garbage bag covering her head.

"Subsequent interviews with Terrence O'Rourke, the neighbor who discovered the body, revealed that on entering the bedroom and finding the victim lying in bed, he tugged at the plastic bag to allow air to enter," he wrote. "It is possible his effort to save her life produced the contusions around her face."

Novak next turned to the initial report of Detective Matt Harris, who assumed responsibility once he arrived. After viewing the scene and turning the immediate examination over to the crime lab and coroner, Harris had crossed the street to interview Terrence and Florence O'Rourke.

Mrs. O'Rourke told how four-year-old Bridey Walsh had appeared at their door at about seven o'clock, barefoot and wearing only a nightgown.

"She was shivering and sobbing," Mrs. O'Rourke said. "I invited her in, but she kept pulling at my robe and trying to tell me something about her mother. I couldn't make out what she was saying, other than that Becky was ill."

She told how she had summoned her husband and, since she was still dressed in nightgown and robe, ordered him to cross the street to investigate. "He didn't want to," she said. "Maybe he didn't think it was proper, entering a woman's house, but the child was hysterical. We had to do something."

So Terrence O'Rourke had entered the house and called out. Hearing no answer, he searched the downstairs and then the upper level. His statement related how he had found the body, been embarrassed by her semi-nude state and so pulled a sheet over her, then tore at the plastic blocking her mouth. "I thought she might still be breathing," he said. "It was a dumb move. I realize that now, but I was in shock and trying to help."

O'Rourke also said that after pulling the sheet over her body, "I realized I was messing up the crime scene, so I pulled it down again."

By then, he said, he had the presence of mind to leave everything else untouched, so he'd run back to his house, told his wife to call the police, gone into the bathroom, and thrown up.

"I've never seen anything like this," he said. "I did my military service in Germany. I've never seen a person killed by a violent act, and we both knew Becky—"

Much of Harris' statement paralleled what Novak had already read, but he described summoning Child Protective Services to remove the four-year-old from the scene, ultimately reuniting her with her grandmother.

Mr. O'Rourke told us that the victim's husband was on a fishing trip at Bessemer Lake. The Boyleston Police Department contacted the Lawrence County Sheriff's Office with instructions to find the husband and notify him of his wife's death. Deputy Michael Garvey reported back within an hour that he had found Mr. Walsh and his companions at the lake's boat launch. When informed about what had occurred, Mr. Walsh broke down. One of his friends offered to drive him back to Boyleston. Mr. Walsh agreed, leaving his car at the lake.

When Walsh arrived, I interviewed him and his friend, Harry Porter. Walsh said that he had spent the entire night with his companions at Beacon Lodge, north of Bessemer Lake. Walsh further claimed he had no idea who had killed his wife and that she had no known enemies. He described their marriage as a happy one.

During the interview, I noticed scratches on Walsh's face, consistent with a physical altercation. Walsh claimed that he had gone through brush and tree limbs at the boat launch and scratched himself.

When I questioned Mr. Porter, he revealed that, contrary to Walsh's claim, he had not spent the night with his companions. While the three had shared a suite at the lodge, Walsh had taken a room in another wing. I later confirmed this with lodge management and took copies of the records.

Porter also said he had noticed scratches on Walsh's face when he arrived at the lodge Friday night.

In speaking with neighbors, I also learned that, far from having a happy marriage, Walsh and his wife were estranged.

On the day following the murder, Deputy Joe Bichsel and I traveled to Bessemer Lake to take possession of Mr. Walsh's vehicle, a 1986 Chevrolet Impala. I drove it back to Pittsburgh, turning it over to the Allegheny County Crime Lab. Among other items, lab technicians found a box of plastic garbage bags and a roll of duct tape in the car's trunk. Tests showed these materials matched the make and gauge of those used to secure the victim and cause her death.

The statement concluded by describing Walsh's arrest and his initial denial of responsibility for his wife's death. He admitted that, after she had suffered a stillbirth months before, their marriage had fallen apart. Walsh stated that they had not had sexual intercourse in six months. He insisted, however, that he still loved his wife and was trying to save their marriage.

The file held three transcripts of interviews with Walsh, but the hour was getting late, so Novak set them aside. He sifted through the remaining documents but was surprised to find no record of interviews with neighbors. He asked the clerk if there might be another box or two. After a brief search, she said, "I've given you everything we have."

"Could anything have been lost or misfiled?"

"No, sir, we've had firm controls over records for years. Everything we have is in those four boxes."

He also questioned her about the county's procedures for booking evidence, satisfying himself that anything gathered was to be turned over at the end of each shift. Harris had not delivered Walsh's vehicle to the county lab until the following afternoon.

Novak returned the files, telling the clerk he would return to listen to the interviews with Walsh. He left dissatisfied, not with what was there, but with what was missing. And not with the evidence against Walsh, thin as it was, but with how it had been gathered.

From his years as a detective, Novak knew this homicide investigation had been sloppy and directed toward a predetermined outcome. The question was what he could do about it.

T wo weeks passed, and the armed robberies were no closer to resolution. County detectives had found only three Honduran immigrants matching the suspect's description, but all had alibis. Questioning of other immigrants had produced no leads. They learned that a pistachio green Vespa motor scooter belonging to a UWV graduate student had been stolen from a carport in Morgan-town, West Virginia in late March. Detectives asked the Morgantown Police Department to look for a Honduran immigrant attending the university or living in the area.

Otherwise, the investigation was at a dead end. The only positive element was that there had been no more holdups. The killer had either been frightened off by his narrow escape from the botched stakeout or had moved on.

On a Monday morning in mid-June, officers arrived to a lingering odor of paint and two bright yellow walls of the bullpen. Mark Ewer stood at his desk, shifting his gaze from one wall to the other. "I was hoping for something in mauve." Even Novak laughed.

He had returned to the ACPD records office twice, reading everything on the murder investigation and listening to recordings of

Thomas Walsh's three interrogations. For hours, the man had maintained his innocence.

> Harris: Tom, we know you did it. Your wife was pregnant by another man—
>
> Walsh: She what?
>
> Harris: You told us you haven't slept with her in more than half a year. Yet she was pregnant. You—
>
> Walsh: You're making that up.
>
> Harris: Here's the autopsy result. (Hands Walsh a report.)
>
> Walsh: I didn't know that.
>
> Harris: She was having an affair with another man. Who was it?
>
> Walsh: (No response.)
>
> Harris: It makes no difference, but you found out about it.
>
> Walsh: No.
>
> Harris: You went up to Bessemer Lake for the weekend, but instead of staying with your buddies, you holed up by yourself.
>
> Walsh: No, I—
>
> Harris: You waited until they turned in for the night, drove home to Boyleston, entered the house, confronted your wife—had you caught her with her lover? Did you wait outside until he'd left?
>
> Walsh: No, I stayed at the lake. They were partying all night, I was working all hours, and needed a good night's sleep.
>
> Harris: You bound her hands and feet with duct tape, tied a plastic bag over her head, and left her there to die. With your little girl sleeping just down the hall. What kind of man lets his four-year-old daughter discover her mother's body?

Until, at the end of a long session in which Matt Harris and another detective had tag-teamed him with the same questions, they made him an offer. "This is capital one—you know that—but if you confess, the DA has promised not to seek the death penalty. You'll get life—there's no avoiding it—but you won't get the chair."

Walsh could be heard sobbing on the tape. Harris bore in.

"Your wife is gone. Your daughter wants nothing to do with you. No friends are visiting. The doors to your business are closed, and creditors are lining up. You have no future here. It's time to come clean."

Again the sound of sobbing, a choked denial.

"It's your life. If you confess. Otherwise..."

And Walsh caved. "All right. I want this to end. Tell me what you want to hear."

Harris led him through a point-by-point description of what he believed had happened, with Walsh responding to each suggestion with a muttered *yes*.

And where was his attorney during all this? By his side. On the verge of bankruptcy, Walsh was represented by a public defender who didn't utter a word during the interrogations.

Novak had no evidence of Walsh's innocence, but neither was he convinced of his guilt.

On the last day of the week, he had a more immediate concern. The city attorney came into his office and shut the door. "We have a situation," he said without preamble.

"McMahon."

Ross nodded. "The good news is that Mrs. Place has decided not to sue. I have no idea what changed her mind. Maybe she's too grief-stricken to go through with it. Perhaps her attorney has decided it's tough to win."

"Or won't take it on contingency." Where lawyers were concerned, Novak was at his most cynical.

"Whatever the reason, we're in the clear."

"But the bad news..." Novak said.

"McMahon's hired an attorney. He's required to submit to arbitration rather than taking us to court, but do you realize how many times cops win these things?"

Novak knew all too well. And Ross' unspoken message was that

Novak might lose the council's support if he were to continue the fight.

"So the bad news is that the good news creates bad news for us," Ross said. "McMahon will argue that, in the absence of a lawsuit, he should be reprimanded, not suspended. He'll demand reinstatement. And he'll win."

"So...?"

"You have to take him back."

Novak folded his arms and locked eyes with the attorney. "I'll resign first."

"No, you won't. If you leave, McMahon wins, and you don't want that. You have to reinstate him, but not as your deputy. He gets the same salary and benefits as before, but you can make him a detective or give him a desk job."

Novak smiled for the first time in their conversation. "Or give him something so demeaning that he'll quit."

Ross waved both hands before him. "You didn't say that, and I didn't hear it."

Novak sunk his face into his hands. "All right, Marv. How do we handle this?"

As Novak arrived home, he heard voices coming from the living room, one of them unfamiliar. He poked his head in, ready to greet a guest, but stopped when he saw a flat black collar with a white border above it. Father Murray turned and favored him with a beatific smile.

"Hello, Karol. Or should I say Chief?"

"Karol will do, Father. Pardon me while I change into mufti."

The priest laughed, but Novak did not. He looked at Barbara and tossed his head to the left, then mounted the stairs. "What is he doing here?" he said as she joined him.

Barbara sighed. "Your mother invited him. She was busy in the kitchen when I got home, preparing what looks to be a feast. Father Tom arrived about fifteen minutes ago."

"It's not your doing," Novak said as he donned a pair of jeans and a T-shirt.

"You'll behave?"

"I don't have a choice. About this or anything else today." He gave her the CliffsNotes version of his conversation with Ross.

"The joys of bureaucracy." As a public employee, she knew the drill.

She left him to finish dressing. Novak radioed the dispatcher to let her know they could reach him at home and slowly made his way down the stairs, gripping the railing.

"Ah, there he is," Father Murray said. "How are you, Karol? We've been worried about you."

"I'm fine, thanks. Fully recovered."

He glared at both Barbara and Izabela, daring them to challenge him. Neither did. In fact, no one spoke for several seconds, with his mother finally breaking the silence. "Dinner is ready. We were just waiting for you."

He muttered something about having a busy day and ushered everyone into the dining room. Barbara had relinquished her throne at the foot of the table so that Novak had to face the priest. His mother brought a steaming bowl of *kapustnica* to the table, and Barbara invited Father Murray to say a blessing. Novak stared straight ahead as he droned on, the aroma of the classic cabbage soup filling the room.

When the priest finally relinquished the floor, Izabela served them, ladling a large serving into each bowl. "This is delicious, Mom," Novak said of the soup he abhorred, having consumed gallons of it as a child.

She smiled and thanked him. "Tell Father Murray about your new job."

"He knows I'm the chief," he said, ignoring her invitation to entertain him with some lurid story.

"How's the morale?" the priest said.

"Improving. They've been through rough times, but they seem grateful for the stability." Though how they would react to McMahon's return was anyone's guess.

"That's good."

"Yes, that is good."

It would have followed for Novak to ask the priest how his flock was faring, but he didn't. Barbara helped Izabela clear the table, and his mother returned with *vyprážaný rezeň* and *bryndzové halušky*, pork schnitzel and dumplings with goat cheese. Novak again complimented his mother, and this time he meant it.

"My anniversary is coming up," Izabela said.

"Oh?" Father Murray said. "Your wedding anniversary?"

"No," she said, a twinkle in her eye, "as you know, I was born in what was then Czechoslovakia."

Novak listened to a story familiar to him and to everyone at the table. He didn't mind hearing it again, as it filled the conversational void.

His mother had been born in Polina, a hamlet in Banská Bystrica, the least populated region of Slovakia. Its principal exports were grain and nuns, along with the occasional priest. Izabela's father, Bedrich Balaz, had left Czechoslovakia in the first months of 1938, when Hitler was demanding the "return" of Sudetenland and any fool could see he would want more.

Bedrich had followed a cousin to Pittsburgh to work in the Jones and Laughlin steel mill, saving every penny he could to bring his wife and daughter to the safety of America.

The Wehrmacht had rolled in faster than his paychecks, however, leaving his family trapped behind enemy lines. Bedrich had been among the first foreign volunteers to enlist in the US Army. He'd fought in North Africa, romped through Sicily without firing a shot, and made the mad rush with Patton's Third Army to liberate Bastogne, where he'd exchanged a finger for a Purple Heart.

When the war in Europe ended, Bedrich had been less than two hundred miles from his wife and child but had no way to reach them, nor had they been aware he was on the continent.

Mother and daughter had finally reached the United States on July 4, 1945, shortly after Izabela's twelfth birthday, on a converted victory ship that carried war brides and other dependents. It anchored in New York Harbor to wait out an impending American holiday. As midnight approached, Izabela had cowered as shells boomed and streams of phosphorus exploded in torrents of fire overhead. Adding to the tumult were the screams of hundreds of women around her, all unaware that America was celebrating its nationhood with a fireworks display.

"The Fourth of July is also my Independence Day," she said. "I came here all those years ago and never left."

"That's literally true," Barbara said. "We took her to see Niagara Falls years ago. We wanted to cross the Peace Bridge to view it from the Canadian side, but there was no way she was going."

"This is my home," she said. "I love America. I'll never leave."

Father Murray clapped, Barbara beamed, and Novak wiped tears from his eyes.

Izabela returned with a version of the Christmas favorite, *Trdelnik*, funnel cake, filled with vanilla ice cream from Bruster's.

All three praised her meal, but as Novak led him to the door, the priest got to the point of the evening. "Karol, you need to attend Mass. Not only for your soul, but for the good of the community. It sends a signal that God is watching over the parish. And I would take it as a personal favor."

"I'm sorry, Father. A month ago, I was unwilling to go; now I cannot."

"You *can't?*" The priest made no effort to hide his confusion. "Why on earth not?"

Novak thought for several seconds before responding. "I took an oath to combat illegality, Father. This church is a criminal enterprise."

McMahon entered the city attorney's office sporting a smug look that suggested he'd just won the lottery. He took a seat and smiled at Novak, who nodded his head. The two turned toward Ross, neither speaking.

"Irene Matola's sister is not pursuing legal action against the department at this time," Ross said.

"She never intended to," McMahon said. "Someone tried talking her into it. I did nothing wrong."

"You violated department policy," Novak said. "If Irene Matola had filed her stay-away order, she might be alive today."

"I didn't say she couldn't."

Nothing will change this jerk. I'm stuck with him.

"Officer, Chief Novak is reinstating you at full pay and benefits—"

"Good." McMahon rose halfway from his chair.

"There are two conditions," Ross said. "First, you are to spend today reviewing the department's policy handbook. When you report tomorrow, we expect you to follow that policy to the letter. No deviations. Is that clear?"

"I always do. What else?"

"The second isn't a condition," Novak said. "It's a reality. You're reinstated at your current salary, but not as my deputy."

He stiffened. "Why not?"

"I need someone in whom I have full confidence. I'm making a change."

McMahon scowled, turning from Novak to Ross and back again. "I don't think you can do that," he said.

"He can. Your rank and salary are one thing, your duties another."

McMahon stared at the attorney for a moment, then took a deep breath. "So, what am I supposed to do, sit around with my thumb up my ass?"

"You're returning as a patrol officer—"

"What?"

"—for the moment," Novak continued. "I will base your future assignments on your performance."

McMahon leaned forward so far he might have fallen into Novak's lap. "I am not going on patrol."

"That's your choice," Ross said. "If you don't accept the assignment, you can resign. It's up to you."

McMahon, his face flushed, stared at the floor for a moment. "We'll see about this." He rose to leave.

"I advise you to return to duty tomorrow morning in a cooperative frame of mind," Ross said. "Your future role is in your hands."

McMahon stormed out without another word. Novak and Ross looked at each other for a few seconds, then Novak left. There was nothing to say.

The day shift was gathering as he entered the bullpen. After Mayfield finished handing out the day's orders, Novak said, "I have a brief announcement. Officer McMahon rejoins us tomorrow. He will initially serve on patrol. I know you'll make him welcome." A few officers looked warily at those alongside them, uncertain how to react.

"I am promoting Sergeant Mayfield and making his appointment as Deputy Chief permanent. Questions? Thank you."

He nodded at the officers and motioned for Barnwell to follow him. "He's back?" she said as Novak closed his office door. "As a patrol officer?"

He offered no explanation. "I'd like you to take on a special assignment, but do so only if you're willing."

"Anything," she said. "What do you need?"

"It's a background investigation. It requires some travel, and I need you to keep it between the two of us."

SCI GREENE WAS a supermax prison due south of Pittsburgh, near the West Virginia line. It was a modern facility, constructed in the early nineties on what had once been farmland. Designated by Greene County as a potential business site, the county's main business was now incarceration. The facility housed the state's most dangerous criminals. A newer united housed those convicted of capital crimes, Thomas Walsh among them.

It took Novak only an hour to drive there, a straight shot down I-79. He registered at the gate, checked his weapon at the reception center, and was escorted to a small conference room used for family visits.

Thomas Walsh shuffled in, looking far older than his sixty-four years. His hair was white, his face was lined with deep creases, his nose was canted to the left, and deep bags drooped below his eyes. From his file, Novak knew another prisoner had attacked him years before. He wore a baggy, maroon uniform with the letters DOC splayed across the back. From Walsh's shambling demeanor, the guard stationed outside the door seemed superfluous.

Seating himself across the table, Walsh removed his glasses and eyed him warily. "You Novak? Why'd you want to see me?"

"I'm looking into your case."

"Why?" He said it without a trace of emotion.

"Your granddaughter asked me to."

"Granddaughter? I've never met her. Why'd she do that?"

"I don't know. So far, her mother won't let me speak to her."

"Bridey?" he said. "I haven't seen her since..." He didn't finish the thought. He probably hadn't set eyes on his daughter since the day he left for Bessemer Lake to join his friends.

"And her daughter's name is...?"

"Amy."

"Amy." Walsh repeated the name as though tasting a strange flavor.

"Why did you refuse to see me for so long?" Novak had been

trying to visit the man for two weeks, but Walsh had turned him down.

"What good can come of it after all this time?"

Novak chose his words carefully. "I'm here in an unofficial capacity. The borough council doesn't know I'm visiting you and wouldn't like it if they found out. But Amy asked my wife to have me look into your conviction, and she nagged me until I did. I'm not satisfied with what I've learned."

"Such as?"

"Let's do this my way. Did you kill your wife?"

He shook his head, as though trying to shake off the memory. "No."

"Did you leave the lodge the night of her murder?"

"I did not. I turned in and slept 'til morning. First good night of sleep I'd had in weeks."

"Why didn't you stay in the same suite as your friends?"

Walsh examined the fingernails of his left hand. "I'd been spending Memorial Day weekend with those guys for as long as I can remember. Ten years. Twelve. Maybe more. Over time, it had come to be less about fishing and more about carousing. That day, I'd worked at the store until closing, so I had to drive up on my own. When I got there, I learned they'd brought in women—whores. We were all married. Me and Becky were having a rough go, and I couldn't afford to get involved in all that. I said thanks but no thanks and took a room of my own."

"You found a vacant room over Memorial Day weekend?"

"Remember what the economy was like back then? I had my pick."

"Why did you lie to the county detectives about your marriage? You told them everything was fine between you."

Walsh snorted. "I was afraid they'd think exactly what they did, that I'd killed her. From the moment that detective started questioning me, he had me in his sights. I hadn't told anyone about our problems. I thought it was between us. Turned out, Becky had blabbed about it. To her *mother*." He spat the word out like a curse.

"Did you know she was involved with another man?"

"No. I was..." His eyes searched the ceiling for an answer. "I spent a lot of time away from the house. The store wasn't doing well, so I laid off the evening shift and manned it myself. I worked twelve hours a day and weekends. Truth is, it was partly to save money and partly to keep clear of Becky. You know she'd lost a baby?"

Novak nodded.

"She blamed me. It wouldn't have happened if I'd been home more. I'd never wanted a second child. I wasn't a good father. On and on she went. It got so I spent as much time away from her as I could. And...I guess she found someone else."

"Who?"

Walsh turned both hands upside down. "No idea."

"Was there anyone she was close to?"

"She was involved at church and in Bridey's preschool. That was about it."

"Did you know she was pregnant?"

"Of course not. If I didn't know she was sleeping around—"

"What would you have done if you'd found out?"

Walsh looked down, stroked his chin. "Who knows? I would have left her, that's for sure. I would have tried to get custody. I loved that little girl. She was..."

Novak waited for him to regain control.

"I wouldn't have killed her, if that's what you mean."

"Why did you confess to something you didn't do?"

"Do you have any idea what it was like? My wife was dead, Becky's mother had my little girl." A scowl crinkled his face. "She's an evil bitch, that one. Acid-tongued, interfering, self-righteous—

"Anyway, I'd lost my family. With me in jail, my business tanked. My friends—none of those guys came to visit, not even a message. I was alone and facing the death penalty. The DA offered me a deal, and Harris and his partner—Albritton, I think his name was—they

wore me down. Hour after hour. Day after day. They even came up
with an inmate who said I'd confessed to him, which I never did. I
didn't even know the guy."

Novak leaned across the table, his voice rising half an octave. "A
jailhouse witness? Do you recall his name?"

Walsh crossed his arms, his face contorting into a scowl. "I'll
never forget it. Dutch name. Gerald Ten Eyck. They dragged him out
of nowhere at my trial. When I appealed, they brought up his testimony. I swear to God, I'd never set eyes on this bastard until he took
the witness stand."

Novak, scribbling, said, "So you gave up?"

"I didn't care anymore. I took the deal and gave them what they
wanted."

Their time was up. Novak promised to return, pledged to
continue looking into the case. Walsh shrugged, as though it no
longer mattered. Then he shuffled back the way he'd come, an old,
broken man.

Novak sat behind the wheel of his cruiser for several minutes,
wondering how much of what Walsh had said was the truth.

As he pulled out of the lot and onto the highway, he passed a
convenience store. A large truck bearing the logo of Norton Food
Services was unloading at the side door. He parked and went inside,
showed his badge and ID to the proprietor, and watched as the driver
made his delivery.

CHAPTER TEN
HE IS ENTITLED TO JUSTICE

Novak had told Lydia Barnwell what he wanted, but not how to get it. "You're the one on the scene. Use your best judgment," he'd said.

While she appreciated the vote of confidence, she was uncertain how to begin, mulling it over during her three-hour drive to the campus of Norwalk State University. Although Novak had struck out, she decided on a frontal assault. It might be more difficult for a fellow officer to refuse an in-person request than that of a disembodied voice on the phone.

Because Novak wanted to keep her absence a secret, she had driven her own car to Norwalk. Nevertheless, she parked in a space marked for *Official Vehicles Only*, entered the police office, flashed her ID to the young man behind the window, and asked for the officer on duty. "Can I tell her what this is about?"

"It's official business."

The man—a student intern, Barnwell suspected—let confusion play across his face before disappearing. He reappeared a moment later and said, "She'll be right with you."

Barnwell waited, trying to conceal her impatience. Five minutes passed, then five more. Finally, the heavy door opened, and a slender, middle-aged woman with salt-and-pepper hair opened the connecting door. She introduced herself as Sergeant Worden—no first name—and said, "How may I help you?"

Barnwell introduced herself, displayed her warrant card, and said, "I'm here for information about a former officer."

"In what connection?"

"May I come in for a moment?"

Worden backed inside and motioned her in with a toss of her head. She led her to a small office in which radio traffic blared. She did not offer Barnwell a seat, but she took one anyway, forcing the sergeant to sit at her desk to keep eye contact.

"Who is this officer, and what information do you need?"

"His name is Daryl McMahon. He worked here between 2010 and 2013 and is now one of our officers. I need to know why he left."

Was there a flash of recognition, or did Barnwell imagine it? "We don't give out personnel information," she said.

"Not even to other law enforcement agencies?"

"We're an independent police force. We don't answer to any other law enforcement unit."

So that was it. A turf war between the campus police and—who? —the city and county?

"I know that," Barnwell said. "That's why I drove all this way." *And this is the most pointless conversation I've had in weeks.*

"I'd appreciate your help," Barnwell said. "Officer McMahon has just returned from suspension. My chief has asked me to look into inconsistencies in his background. All I'm asking is why he left."

"I'm not authorized to provide that kind of information. Perhaps the university's HR department can assist you. Would you like a map of the campus?"

Barnwell declined the offer, saying she could find her own way. As they left her office, Barnwell handed her a business card. "If you change your mind, here's my phone number."

She turned at the door. "Daryl McMahon put a lot of women in danger. One lost her life because of his negligence. Chief Novak has been forced to return him to duty, but he needs to know if there's anything in his background that's a cause for concern. You could help."

"I'm sorry," Worden said.

Barnwell left, sitting in her car while considering her next step. She had spoken her closing words to Worden in the open on the chance that other officers might hear. She hoped the seeds she'd thrown would reach fertile ground.

"Bingo!" Calvin Mayfield entered the office without knocking, his right thumb thrust into the air. "You were right."

Novak smiled and leaned back in his chair. "Tell me."

"Just as you said, Norton makes all the sandwiches and baked goods itself, but it contracts the packages of fruits and vegetables to Moretti and Sons down in the Strip. They're a produce wholesaler, selling mainly to independent grocery stores. They also prep wrapped fruit and vegetable trays, including the individual packs you spotted down in Waynesburg."

"And someone has to peel the carrots and core the apples," Novak said, "the sort of job companies hire migrants to do."

"Or illegals."

"Nice work, Detective. Let's let our friends at County know."

The offices of the *Norwalk Daily*, the campus newspaper, were on the second floor of the Media Arts building. Barnwell introduced herself and asked to see the October and November 2013 issues.

"We no longer keep print copies," a journalism student told her. "Everything's electronic. You log on to our site, go to the archive page, and pick the year, month, and date."

Since she lacked either a computer or an account, the student placed her at an empty workstation and logged on with guest credentials.

"What are you looking for?" he asked.

"I'm not certain, and even if I find something, I may not recognize it. Can you show me how to go about this?"

He led her through the process, then left her alone, although, like any good reporter, he kept glancing in her direction.

The newspaper was a daily, and it not only covered campus events, but community and national stories as well. At first, this made for slow going, requiring her to look through every issue. She soon realized that any campus news, apart from sporting events, was contained on the first three pages, making her search much easier.

She had just finished skimming all the October issues when her cell phone rang. The caller ID read "No Listing." Assuming it was spam, she pushed the red circle to ignore it. She continued searching, but her phone rang again. Once more, she ignored it.

On the third ring, she picked it up, listening without speaking. "I know you're there." A man's voice. Not one she recognized, and yet...

"Leave it alone. Go back to Pittsburgh. This is fair warning." He disconnected.

She scratched at the glass surface of the phone, found her call history, and tried to redial the last number. Nothing happened. There was no number.

"Everything all right?" the student said.

"Spam. I can't put a stop to these damned calls."

"There's an app that blocks a lot of them. It costs a bit, but it's worth it. Let me show you."

"That's okay. Maybe later."

She resumed her search with renewed determination. The stupid jerk had just confirmed that McMahon had something to hide, but she reached the end of November without finding a clue what it could be.

There was a gap over the Thanksgiving holiday, so she took a chance and began reading the December issues. On December 3, she found it. She'd seen related stories over the past month, but they'd made no sense to her at the time. Now, everything fell into place.

"Can I print articles?" she asked. She chose an innocuous story as the student demonstrated. The central printer was one desk away from his, so anything she chose, he could see. She selected another story, committed it to print, and strode to the printer to grab it. She returned to the workstation and chose another, repeating the process three more times.

He pretended to ignore her, but she was aware that he watched her every move. *What do I care if a campus newspaper outs a scumbag police officer who's lied about his past?*

She thanked him and gathered up her papers.

"Let me ask you something."

Here it comes. "Yes?"

"Are you free for dinner tonight?"

She chuckled and showed him her perfect teeth. "I'd like nothing better, but I can't stay. I'm heading down to Doubleday."

THE RAID WENT DOWN AS PLANNED. ICE agents executed a warrant on Moretti and Sons, detaining eight workers, releasing four after they produced papers, but holding the rest. They seized the company's employment records but did nothing to the managers who had hired workers who should not have been in the United States.

Novak felt a twinge of guilt that the four had been ensnared in a net meant to catch someone else. They had hurt no one, weren't living off taxpayers, and were doing jobs that no one else cared to do. They were victims.

Novak and Mayfield joined Detective Carpenter in the manager's office after the immigration officers had departed.

"We're not interested in these people," Carpenter began. "There's one guy we're trying to find. He's armed and dangerous. He's committed several armed robberies and one murder. If you know who he is and fail to tell us, I promise you'll do jail time. I will see to it."

The manager, Manny Ricci, gulped and nodded. Carpenter described the suspect, mentioning that he rode a green Vespa.

"That's Aaron," he said. "Aaron Ramos. At least that's what he calls himself. We fired him three months ago. He's a druggie. Unreliable. One of the crew said—after he'd left, of course—that he'd stolen a truck over on South Side a few months back and wrecked it. Ran from the scene. They didn't catch him, but he was unlicensed—"

"Illegal?" Carpenter said.

"I'm not sure. I don't ask. Anyway, he drives a green motor scooter. No car, no license, but he has to get around, doesn't he?"

"Where does he live?" Novak said.

"How would I know?"

"Where did you send his checks?" Mayfield asked.

Carpenter snorted. "Our friend here paid him in cash. Not even minimum wage. No paperwork. No records. No FICA. Five, six bucks an hour and all the celery he could eat, right?"

Ricci didn't answer.

"Who would know?" Novak said.

The man shrugged.

"Let's call the feds back in," Carpenter said.

"Maybe one of the other guys keeps in touch," the man said, suddenly accommodating.

Carpenter made a sweeping motion with his right arm. *After you,* it said.

It took fifteen minutes to question the workers, not because they were uncooperative, but because one of the four had to translate for the others. When the officers left, however, they not only knew the identity of the perpetrator, but also, within one city block in The Shanties, where he was staying.

"Have you heard from Officer Barnwell?"

Norma Showalter turned from her computer and faced him. "No, sir, was I supposed to?"

"Just tell me the minute she calls."

Now that was stupid. Entering his office, Novak removed his jacket and weapon. *If she calls, she'll tell Norma to interrupt me.*

He looked up as David Kimrey entered without knocking and closed the door behind him. "I haven't heard from her, either. This isn't like her."

The closed door in her apartment. The toilet flushing. Lydia's devious explanation that the apartment walls were thin.

"How much has she told you?"

"Just that she was doing something for you and would be gone a couple days. I expected her back last night."

Novak had too. He'd also expected Barnwell to call him to report whether or not she had found anything, but he'd heard nothing. No call. No text. He held his cell phone in his hand but didn't know whom to call.

"She didn't tell you what she was doing?"

"No. She said it was confidential."

"Have you told anyone else?"

"No, what is there to tell? I mean, a couple people asked where she is."

Novak stroked his cheek with the phone. "And you told them...?"

"That she was out of town working on something."

"David, David, who did you tell?"

"Ewer asked. You know how he is. Wants to be everyone's buddy."

"No one else? Someone standing around who might have overheard you?"

"No," he said. "What are we going to do?"

Novak opened his phone and began paging through it. "Leave it to me. I'm calling in a favor. Stay strong. And ping her phone."

"I already have. It's been dead for hours, but the last signal was

Monday night from a tower near Ohio Route 61, just south of Norwalk."

Novak tried to conceal his sense of panic as Kimrey rose, dejected, then paused at the door. "Open or closed?"

"Close it. No, wait a minute. Get Ewer in here."

He fiddled with his phone while he waited, finding a contact and tagging it as a favorite. Ewer entered, buoyant as ever. "What's up, Chief? Beautiful morning. Summer's here—"

"Shut the door," Novak said.

Ewer did as directed, then faced him, still wearing a silly-ass grin.

"Monday afternoon, you asked Officer Kimrey where Barnwell was."

"Yeah. I know they're shacked up. Everyone does. Best thing that's ever happened—"

"Why did you ask? Isn't she allowed a day off?"

Ewer dropped his smile for the first time in Novak's memory. "Is something wrong?"

"Answer my question, Detective. Why did you ask where she was, and who did you tell?"

A knock at the door. "Chief?" Norma Showalter said.

"Not now."

"Chief, it's important."

Lydia. Novak stood and opened his door. "I'm sorry to interrupt, but it's Councilman Lentz. I explained you were in a meeting, but he told me to interrupt you."

"All right, tell him to hold. I'll just be a minute."

Slamming the door. Turning to Ewer. "Make it quick. Who did you tell?"

"McMahon," he said. "He asked me to find out."

Novak's sigh of exasperation was so loud that Ewer took a step back. "What's wrong?"

Idiot! "Leave. Close the door. And for God's sake, don't tell anyone I asked. Keep your mouth shut, if you can."

He sat at his desk for ten seconds, forcing himself to relax. "Chief Novak," he said into the office phone.

"This is Doug Lentz. Something serious has come up. The council wants to meet with you in closed session after tomorrow night's regular meeting."

"What's this about?"

"We'll discuss it tomorrow night."

"I may not make it. We have some serious shit coming down—"

"Be there. That's an order."

Lentz hung up, leaving Novak staring at his closed door. The room began to spin. He tried to focus on the coat hook, but saw two images he couldn't resolve.

Oh, God, no. Not again. He leaned forward, resting his head on outstretched arms, feeling his heart race.

"I'LL DO IT," Calvin Mayfield said. "No one will notice one more brother in the hood."

"Not alone," Novak said. "I'm your backup." *I have one officer missing and will not lose another.*

"You guys are sure?" Carpenter said. "It's our case. We should handle this."

"We live and work here," Mayfield said. "We know this neighborhood better than anyone."

The Shanties comprised six blocks of narrow row houses, thrown up overnight years before by a local steel mill to house its workers. A century later, some were occupied despite leaking roofs and missing bricks, a few were gone, now just vacant lots, and many were abandoned and ruled uninhabitable. The homeless, whores, and addicts had commandeered several of them, scratching out an existence without water, light, or heat.

"On Romberg, near Cedar." That's what one of the Central American workers had told them, but which abandoned eyesore he couldn't say. So Novak and Mayfield made their way down the alley south of Romberg Avenue in the twilight, looking for signs of life. Carpenter stood by with a SWAT team at the end. Other officers were stationed at the corner on Romberg and Cedar, ready to move in.

This was not how they typically handled a raid, but since the team didn't know which house the killer was using, they had to narrow the search. Were they to storm into the wrong one, their racket would alert their quarry.

Novak wished Barnwell had been present Monday afternoon to interview the laborer in Spanish. They might have gotten more precise information. At the moment, he'd give anything just to know where she was.

All day, he'd tried to hide his apprehension from the men, but as word got around, he could feel the tension within the department. Adding to his anxiety was the knowledge that he was responsible. He had sent Barnwell alone on this mission—an unofficial investigation that might have nothing to do with legitimate law enforcement concerns. If something happened to her, he wouldn't need the council to cut his balls off. He'd do it himself.

Highway patrolmen in three states had her description and that of her car. The Ohio Highway Patrol had retraced her steps at NSU. Novak had pulled every string he could think of, with no result. That evening, the hunt for Adi Patel's killer was a welcome diversion.

Vandals had broken all the windows in the third row house in the alley, but because the back porch had collapsed, they couldn't look inside for signs of occupation. They crept forward. The second abandoned house, near the opposite end of the block, had a garage in back and what looked like blankets covering the windows. Mayfield turned and smiled at him. Novak nodded toward the garage. Mayfield directed the beam of his flashlight through a broken window.

A dog barked on a back porch across the alley. "Shit," Mayfield whispered.

"Get away from there!" In the dim light, Novak made out a figure standing on the porch. "What are you up to?" The dog echoed his master's voice.

Novak reached for his badge, but at that moment, the man raised his arm and fired. Novak whirled and crouched. "Police," he cried, "drop your—"

A second shot drowned out his words. Mayfield's breath exploded in a loud *whoosh* as he dropped onto his back. Novak raised his .38 and fired as the SWAT team raced up the alley toward them. Novak fired again, shouting, "Police!"

The gunman dropped his rifle, his hands in the air. The SWAT team reached the back gate, stormed through the small yard and up the stairs, while Novak kneeled over Mayfield.

"Calvin, buddy. Talk to me. Officer down!" he shouted into his microphone. "Need help now!"

A medical officer ran toward them. Behind him, Novak heard a small engine fire, the sound growing louder as it rounded the back of the garage toward the alley. Novak sprung toward the scooter as it emerged and turned away from him. He grabbed for the handlebar, the force nearly tearing his arm from its socket. But the back tire slid, the motorbike toppled and spun in a complete circle, and the rider slid off, striking two trash cans behind the adjacent garage.

As the rider struggled to his feet, Novak reached for his weapon, covering the ten yards in six long steps. "You are under arrest."

Hearing the commotion, two members of the SWAT team broke off and handcuffed the suspect, while Novak returned to his downed officer.

"How is he?"

The medic began to reply, but Mayfield interrupted him. "I'm okay. My chest hurts like hell, but I'm okay."

"The vest," the medic said. "It stopped the bullet. He may have a busted rib or two, but he'll be all right. We'll get him to a hospital to check him over."

The medic radioed for an ambulance, parked only a block away during the raid as a precaution. Novak leaned against the garage with one hand as he vomited.

"Are you all right?" the medic asked.

"No. Not at all."

NOVAK'S CELL phone rang as he got home two hours later. "Novak," he said.

"Hi, Karol. It's Randy Stebbins. Good news. We found her."

"Where? How?" he asked the Ohio State Patrol captain. "Is she all right?"

"She's fine. Tired, angry, but okay. She's in jail. Or was."

"Where? On what charge?"

"A small-town police chief stopped her for speeding Monday night. Because she's out of state, they demanded she post a cash bond. When she couldn't, they held her for trial."

"Randy, we don't jail people for—"

"Neither do we. It's a local scam. We just got her free, so I don't yet have details. We've put her up at a local motel until morning. She wants someone to come get her."

Novak promised to come himself, then called David Kimrey to give him the news. He picked up the officer at 5:30 the following morning, and the two headed north to the Turnpike, then west past Cleveland and into Northwest Ohio.

As they rode, Novak related what little he knew. As soon as he had ended his call from Lentz the previous morning, he'd called Stebbins, a classmate at Pitt with whom he'd worked on three cross-border cases over the years. The OHP officer had taken personal charge of the search, beginning with Barnwell's last known location before her cell phone went dead.

The OHP found her car at a county impound lot, through which they traced her to a rural police station south of Norwalk. The night officer refused to release her from their two-cell lockup without authorization from the chief, who had made the arrest and then made himself hard to find.

But find him they did, and when he refused to release Barnwell into Stebbins' custody, he called the county DA, who wielded considerably more influence. Barnwell was distraught and exhausted, having slept little during the past two nights. After putting her up in a cheap motel, Stebbins promised to alert Novak.

Now, here they were. Lydia awaited them in the breakfast room of the motel. Kimrey embraced her, but they showed no more affection in front of Novak.

"I need to pick up my car," she said after assuring them she was unharmed. "My suitcase is still in the trunk. I'm wearing the same clothes I had on when I left. And the bastard took my cell phone."

Their fight wasn't over. The manager of the impound lot wouldn't release her vehicle without an order from the chief, who didn't respond to Novak's call. He called Stebbins, who called the district attorney, who called the lot manager, who responded with a string of yes-sir-right-away-sir's.

"I want out of this freaking town," Lydia said. "David, drive my car back. I'm going with the chief."

"You two can go together," Novak said. "We'll catch up tomorrow."

"Hell, no. We're going to Doubleday," she said. "We're going to finish this assignment."

Novak was to meet with the council in several hours, but as they drove south and Barnwell chattered nonstop, he realized this was more important. She told him what she'd learned...and what she suspected.

HE'D CALLED AHEAD to warn Lentz he might be late. "Fifteen minutes," the council president said. "No more."

"I'll get there when I get there, and you will listen." Novak disconnected before he could argue.

He made it with ten minutes to spare, but half the council members were late. Novak scrawled notes on a legal pad as he waited for them to assemble. When finally they closed the doors of the small chamber, Lentz glared at him, still smarting from his impertinence. "Nice of you to join us," he said.

"This has been a busy day. I traveled five hundred miles to make it here. I assume it's important."

"You're damned right," Councilman Frain said.

"Hold on, Byron. I call the Boyleston Borough Council together for a closed session. Clerk will call the roll."

"We're all here," Frain said.

Ignoring the interruption, the chairman had the clerk intone the name of each member.

He first asked Novak to report on the arrest of the armed robbery suspect.

After summarizing the previous night's action, he said, "The county is holding Aaron Ramos on charges of armed robbery, homicide, and several lesser charges. He's an addict and is held in isolation at Mercy, so County has been unable to question him. Until they do, we won't know why he robbed these specific convenience stores or what their connection is to his termination by Moretti."

"And Sergeant Mayfield?" Bernie Jackson asked.

"He has two fractured ribs and a bruised ribcage, but no internal injuries." *And no concussion.* "He's in good spirits and expects to return Monday."

Lentz asked Novak to pass along the council's condolences and acknowledged the department's role in ending the suspect's reign of violence. "All right, Byron," he said. "You and Mayor Tifton asked for this meeting. Proceed."

"Why didn't you reinstate Daryl McMahon as Deputy Chief?" Frain said, leaning forward like a grand inquisitor.

Novak glanced at Bernie Jackson. When they'd spoken the afternoon before, the councilman had not yet learned the reason for the executive session, but Novak had assumed that Frain and Tifton were behind it and that McMahon was the subject.

"I reinstated him to his full rank and salary, which, I might add, was uninterrupted during his suspension. He's had a nice vacation at taxpayer expense."

"You did not reinstate him as Deputy Chief."

"No, I did not. Nor will I."

"That's what we're here to decide," Frain said.

"No, you're not. As soon as I've met with the city attorney, I'm terminating his employment."

No one spoke until Tifton broke the silence. "On what grounds?"

"Daryl McMahon concealed material facts from the borough when he applied."

Tifton was momentarily stunned into silence. "What facts?" Lentz said.

"From 2010 to 2013, Daryl McMahon was employed by the police force at Norwalk State. During that time, several female students complained of his inappropriate advances. The police chief investigated but didn't act. In the fall of 2013, two women reported that McMahon forced them to engage in sex after he found marijuana in their possession. They came forward only after a third student refused another demand and went directly to the university. Norwalk State settled with the three students in return for their signing nondisclosure agreements. They allowed McMahon to resign, all to keep it out of the local press."

Novak looked at each council member in turn to be sure he had their attention.

"For over six months, he was unemployed, eventually landing a low-paying job as chief of the Doubleday police force, supervising two part-time officers. There, two women accused him of forcing them into sex acts, one after he discovered her dealing amphetamines, the other after he stopped her for driving under the influence with a small child in back. The town council fired him, but

Doubleday is so small it no longer has a local newspaper to report it."

The only sound came from Councilwoman Lunate, who heaved a sigh with each new revelation.

"Like the university, Doubleday concealed the reason for his termination, avoiding a potential lawsuit while passing their problem on to whoever might hire him next. That allowed McMahon to move here and gain certification as a Pennsylvania law enforcement officer. When we confronted Doubleday's mayor this afternoon, he not only opened his files but also revealed that Chief Russell had contacted him two years before."

"This was prior to hiring him?" Lentz asked.

"It was." Like a Sunday preacher, Novak raised his hands to emphasize what he was about to say. "Russell knew McMahon's background but hired him because he was useful. McMahon ran the department, leaving Russell to focus on his side business. McMahon covered for Russell in exchange for his professional redemption."

Novak told them that, after noticing gaps in McMahon's employment history, he'd assigned Lydia Barnwell to investigate. He described her discovery of stories in the NSU student newspaper about a sex scandal involving an unnamed officer, the anonymous phone call warning her to leave, and her arrest as she drove south toward Doubleday.

"The anonymous caller's voice sounded familiar to her. During our drive back, we confirmed that Daryl McMahon's older brother, Damon, heads the university's patrol division. We can imagine the sequence of events. Damon called his brother to tell him we were on campus asking questions. They arranged for her arrest with a friendly police chief, telling him to hold her incommunicado until tonight's meeting, at which I was to be fired and replaced by McMahon."

Novak folded his hands prayerfully and waited for someone to speak.

Bernie Jackson filled the void. "Incredible," he said. "I trust no member of the council was a party to this."

"Absolutely not," Frain said. "This is inexcusable." All the others muttered their agreement, while Jackson rolled his eyes toward Frain.

"On behalf of the council," the chairman said, "I apologize for the misunderstanding. This has been a great week for the department. We're all in your debt. If there's nothing else..."

"I'm not finished," Frain said.

Lentz drummed his fingers on the council table. "It's getting late."

"When we met last week, Mayor Tifton asked if you were looking into a cold case. You denied this. I'm informed—"

"That's not true," Novak said.

"Let me finish."

"I did not deny looking into it. I said I was not distracted. I wasn't." Rapping the table with his knuckles for emphasis, he said, "*We* solved these armed robberies. Not the county. This department. I have done my duty despite constant interference and second-guessing."

"What is this case?" Frain's hands shook, and he sprayed spittle across the table as he shouted at Novak.

"The murder of Rebecca Walsh in May 1989. I was asked to look into it. I did so on my own time and, apart from asking our detectives for anything they might recall about it, used no departmental resources."

"It's a closed case," Tifton said. "Thomas Walsh was investigated, arrested, tried, and convicted. He even confessed. It's over."

"I have serious questions about that investigation. Walsh was a prominent citizen of this borough, a business leader and family man. If he was wrongfully convicted, we have a duty to bring him justice."

"The courts dispensed justice," Tifton said.

"They may not have in his case."

"Enough, Fred," Lentz said. "Karol, you're the chief. If you need to look into this matter, you may do so as long as it doesn't interfere with your duties."

Novak nodded, but Frain spoke again. "Mr. Chairman, this man accused Deputy McMahon of concealing his background, and I agree it's serious. But he wasn't forthcoming with us. I've learned the Pittsburgh Police Department forced him to retire due to a medical condition."

"Fred, shut up!" Although he sat at the opposite end of the table, Councilman Jackson was in the mayor's face.

"He lied—"

"He did not. I was on the search committee, as were Chairman Lentz and Councilwoman Lunate. Karol fully disclosed his medical condition. He had an injury and was treated for it. He provided all his records. His physician met with us and cleared him for duty."

"You never revealed this," Frain said.

"Why would we? His doctor says he's able." No longer the neutral mediator, Lentz was now in the fight.

Frain shook his head, but Tifton said, "He hasn't told his officers."

"What do they need to know?" Jackson said. "If he broke his leg and recovered, would he have to give everyone the details?"

Through all this, Novak sat at the small desk alongside the clerk, resting his head in his hands, covering his eyes.

"Perhaps he should do that," Lentz said, reverting to his role as peacemaker. "Chief, are you willing to share this information with your staff?"

Novak raised his head, conscious that all eyes were focused on him. "Yes," he said, his voice just above a whisper.

"Then it's decided. Chief Novak will meet with his officers and disclose his past condition. The council continues to have confidence in him."

Amid mutters of agreement, Novak said, "That's no longer the question."

"I'm sorry?"

Novak rose to his feet. "It's not whether *you* have confidence in *me*, but whether *I* have confidence in *you*."

He left without another word.

THOMAS WALSH

CHAPTER ELEVEN
THE MAN WITH NO MEMORY

Barbara's voice rose, reflecting her disbelief. "You said what?"

Novak repeated his parting shot.

"Was that wise?"

"Remember what you told me. The council needs me more than I need them."

She reached her hand across the breakfast table. "I did say that, didn't I? For once, you listened."

"And frankly, my dear, I no longer give a damn."

Izabela had watched television until well after midnight and had slept in again, allowing them time to discuss the efforts of some council members to undermine him.

"I can't figure out why Tifton opposes my looking into the Walsh case. We caught Patel's killer, so the few hours I spent on it didn't sidetrack us one bit."

"It's about control. He's frustrated because he's no longer in charge."

"After last night, he won't ever be."

"So now you're free to look into it."

"Yes, and I will. And I'll have help. Speaking of which, seeing as how you have the whole summer off—"

He knew how that rankled. "Okay, smartass, tell me what you need."

After asking Barbara to conduct some research for him, Novak left for work, ready for the confrontation that lay ahead, but McMahon didn't show up. Novak pictured the panicky back-and-forth when Damon discovered Barnwell had been released. So concerned were the Brothers McMahon for their own skins that they hadn't thought to alert Tifton, allowing him to walk into a trap at the council meeting.

Marvin Ross would notify McMahon of his termination. The ACPD would make certain that he never again served in law enforcement in the commonwealth. Ohio's attorney general would investigate the actions of his brother and the small-town police chief who had arrested Barnwell.

At eight o'clock, the seam between the night and day shifts, Novak gathered the officers together in the bullpen. Barnwell was present, haggard but upbeat. As her fellow officers welcomed her back, Novak said, "I didn't expect to see you."

"What do you think I am, a fragile flower? I'm a police officer."

"Yes, you are. All right, everyone, gather 'round." He began by giving them the latest on Mayfield's condition. "He's being released from the hospital today, he'll spend the weekend in bed, and he expects to return Monday for light duty. No more alley fights for a while."

Their laughter could not hide the underlying tension. One of their officers had essentially been kidnapped while another had come under fire. Like law enforcement officers everywhere, they were not just a team, but a family.

His announcement that McMahon would not return brought smiles of relief. He didn't explain why, nor did they seem to expect him to. Personnel matters were confidential, and he knew they had ways of uncovering the story without putting their chief in an untenable position.

He made a few more desultory announcements, delaying the

inevitable for as long as possible. "I have something important to tell you." He glanced around the room. Did they already know what he was about to say? McMahon had found a source in the Pittsburgh Police Department. Was Tifton the only one with whom he'd shared Novak's secret?

"As many of you know, I love football—not the kind *you* follow, but the real kind, the kind you play with your feet." A few sniggers around the room.

"I played in high school and for Pitt, and I continued to play in amateur leagues for years. I was a keeper—goalkeeper, like in hockey?" Again a few laughs.

"And I was a damned good one. That ended two summers ago. We were playing against Carnegie. Their right winger dribbled the ball to the corner. He lofted a cross shot to a forward, who got past two defenders and passed it to an incoming midfielder." He halted for a moment, reliving what others had told him about what followed.

"He headed the ball toward the net. I blocked it, sprawled forward, and covered it with my arms." He demonstrated, leaning forward, arcing his arms before him.

"The midfielder thought the ball might come back out, so he slid toward me, feet first, right into my head. I suffered a concussion. I was off work for two weeks. When I returned, I had balance problems. My vision got blurry. My attention wandered. The worst thing was the memory lapses."

Barnwell sighed. "That Czech goalkeeper."

"Yeah, Petr Čech, my role model. You may have seen his photo in my office. He suffered the same injury. He came back. *And so have I.*"

He let that sink in. "I still have occasional balance problems. When I'm under pressure, I sometimes get double vision—rarely, but it happens. I have a bit of trouble remembering things. Nothing important, just details. It's like losing peripheral vision. You see what's in front of you but not off to the side.

"So I take notes. We all do when we're on a crime scene. It's part of our DNA, right? I have to do it constantly to make sure I don't miss anything."

He looked into their faces, trying to peer past their grave expressions to divine their thoughts. "The search committee knew this when they hired me. They know I've been through months of occupational therapy. My doctor signed off on my ability to do this job."

He looked aside for a moment, wondering whether to self-censor, then plunged ahead. "The council reaffirmed their support last night. I hope I have yours."

"Hell, yes," Ewer said. "You're the best chief ever."

Others chimed in, and Novak, thankful for once for Ewer's irrepressible enthusiasm, realized they'd been readying themselves for something entirely different. They'd expected him to announce his departure.

"Okay," he said, silencing their reactions with outstretched hands, "if we're going to make this work, I'll need your support. Here's where we'll begin."

He'd LAID out his doubts about the Walsh case. "The investigation was a travesty. They compromised the crime scene from the outset. The investigating officer focused on the victim's husband, ignoring everything else. He never interviewed neighbors. He broke the evidentiary chain of custody and may have corrupted it; he was later dismissed by the county for doing just that in drug cases. We will do what he should have done. We'll go back to the beginning and do this right."

Officers who had previously been sitting at their desks had clustered around him to catch every word. "Some of you will be directly involved in this investigation. I depend on the rest to cover everything else going on in the borough. It will be like the early days of the armed robbery investigation, only this time we have one crime, one victim, and one focus."

He had felt their excitement. For the second time in two months, they would conduct real investigative work, not just handing the meatiest cases over to Allegheny County. And Novak was happier than he'd been since he got back into harness. There were no longer constraints on his authority. He could investigate the Walsh murder in the open.

Now, as he sat across the conference table from Thomas Walsh again, he said, "We're devoting our full attention to your case. I need you to be completely honest. Hold nothing back, even if you think it hurts your case. Do that for us, and we'll do everything we can for you."

Walsh blinked, stared at Novak for a moment, and smiled—the first time he'd done that in Novak's presence. "Thank you."

"I don't want to raise your hopes too—"

"I know," Walsh said. "You don't need to tell me nothing may come of it. But to have someone willing to even take a look..." He raised his hands toward the heavens, allowing the sentence to finish itself.

Novak took him back to the months before the murder. In November of 1988, seven months into her second pregnancy, Becky had miscarried due to insufficient blood flow to the placenta. The fetus was a male. Walsh had named him Michael and arranged for his burial. His wife had not taken part in the arrangements and had stood by the gravesite, displaying no emotion. In the weeks that followed, depression had settled over her like a shroud. "I tried to get her to see our family doctor, but she insisted she was fine, that I was the problem. She stopped speaking to me, and whenever she did, she was hostile."

He kneaded his hands together, his look that of a little boy pleading to be believed. "Like I said last time, I buried myself in my work. You remember how the economy was back then, the recession, all those Fortune 500 companies leaving Pittsburgh. People weren't buying anything. I had all this inventory sitting around, bought on my line of credit. The bank nagged me in the morning and Becky in the evening, and I just—I about moved into the store."

Walsh insisted he had no idea his wife had a boyfriend, had been unaware she was two months pregnant, and knew no one who might have fathered the child. "We were a churchgoing couple. There'd been no one else in our lives. We were devoted to each other—at least until she lost the baby."

He looked at the ceiling. "One day, we were the happiest little family you can imagine. The next, things fell apart. I could see it happening, like leaves falling from a tree until there were just bare branches and ugly twigs."

"Thomas—"

"Tom. You can call me Tom."

"Tom, the most damning evidence was the roll of duct tape and the box of industrial strength garbage bags in the trunk of your car. Your prints were all over them."

"I didn't put them there."

"How did they get there?" Novak said, though he suspected he knew the answer.

"I have no idea. I kept stuff like that in a closet off the dining room. Becky was always on me to clean it out."

Novak asked him to relate everything he remembered from the weekend of his wife's murder. How had she seemed when he left? Did she mention any plans? Walsh's answers provided no hint of what had led someone to kill her.

"When Harris brought you in for questioning, you had deep scratches on your face. You told him you'd cut through brambles at the boat launch, but his report said the area was devoid of vegetation. One of your companions told him your face was scratched when you arrived, so you changed your story, saying you'd fallen at your store while moving a heavy item. Is that true?"

Walsh looked down but said nothing.

"Tom, if I'm to help you, you'll have to level with me. That's the deal."

Closing his eyes, he stroked the tip of his nose with the fingers of his left hand. "Becky," he said in a quiet voice.

"She did that?"

"We had a disagreement—okay, a fight—while I was about to leave for the lake. 'You're not going fishing. You're never here.' On and on. When I insisted, she reached out and clawed me. It happened so fast, it took me by surprise."

"Then what?"

"Then nothing. I turned around and left. Got in my car and drove north."

"Did you defend yourself? Reach out? Take a swing at her?"

Walsh was forceful in his denials. Novak threw questions at him, challenging him, asserting it would have been natural to fight back. Walsh insisted he'd done nothing. "I just left, like I said. It was the last time I saw her. Or Bridey."

"Your daughter saw this?"

"Yeah, hiding behind her mother." He closed his eyes as though picturing the scene.

"Tom, is there anything else you told investigating officers, the court, your own attorney, that is untrue? Anything at all. I have to know."

"Nothing. The only things I twisted were about our relationship. Harris was after me. He'd already decided I'd killed her. I didn't want to give him ammunition."

And yet he had. Novak ran a hand through his hair, trying to decide if he believed the man, considering what to ask next. "Another issue is your lack of an alibi. Are you certain no one can vouch for you?"

"Yeah, I was alone."

"Did you call Becky from the hotel?"

"No, not after that send-off. I had a late dinner on my own, watched TV for a while, and went to bed."

Novak drummed his fingers. Time was getting short, and he

needed something—anything—to open a crack in this closed door. He questioned Walsh again on why he'd confessed.

Tears came to the man's eyes. "You know what I said about my world falling apart? Before Becky's murder, I had a family, a beautiful little daughter I doted on, customers who'd been with me for years, and friends. Boy, did I have some good friends. People I'd known since grade school."

He broke off, unable to speak. "Take your time," Novak said.

Walsh struggled to regain his composure. "I had nothing. I'd lost my business. No one came to see me, not even my three buddies, the guys who were with me while we launched the boat Saturday morning. They knew I couldn't have done this. They never came, never called...

"So when those detectives offered the deal—my life for my confession—I just gave up."

He lowered his voice. "After the trial, I woke up in here one morning and thought, 'what have I done?' What *have* I done? But it was too late."

"I've read the trial transcript," Novak said. "A weak part of your defense was the fact that you booked a separate room at the last minute. The prosecution tied all these pieces together in a damning package. Just before you leave for your fishing trip, you find out your wife is pregnant by another man. You two are having problems, your business is in trouble, a divorce will ruin you, and you may lose your daughter. So you drive your own car up to the lake rather than traveling with your friends, book your own room, drive back to Boyleston, kill your wife, return to the lake, grab a few hours of sleep, and show up for breakfast."

"That's not what happened."

"Tell me again."

"I drove separately because I had to work late. When I arrived, I learned they'd brought prostitutes along. Or maybe they were local girls. I don't know. I wanted no part of it, so I booked my own room."

"Tom, why didn't your lawyer bring this out? A good defense attorney puts everyone else on trial."

"They asked me not to. All three were married. It would have ruined them. They passed word through the public defender, begging me not to disclose the details. There was a veiled threat behind it. Don't tell on us, or we'll make things rough for you."

"What did they mean by that?"

"I have no idea. They were desperate. Maybe they were going to make something up."

"Which 'friend' sent that message? Do you recall?"

"I sure do."

Walsh gave him a name. Novak stared at him, mouth agape.

DETECTIVE MATT HARRIS had pushed himself into the Walsh investigation. Andrew Millar, the ACPD detective who'd arrived first at the Walsh home, had described to Novak how Harris had barreled in twenty minutes after Millar's arrival and assumed control.

"I was newly minted, and he had several years on me," Millar told Novak. "He took over. Paid no attention to the information I'd gathered. Just started questioning that couple—"

"Terrence and Florence O'Rourke," Novak prompted.

"That's it. What a couple. Little guy, big woman. A Mutt and Jeff act."

Novak laughed. "I have an officer looking for them."

"Anyway, it was like I wasn't there. 'Get outta my way, kid.' Know what I mean?"

Novak could picture the scene. Harris breezing in, sizing up the situation, sensing an easy arrest, and nudging his young colleague aside. And then, cocksure of himself, focusing the investigation on the most likely suspect, leaving all other avenues unexplored.

But the fact that Harris had mishandled the probe—perhaps even manufactured evidence—did not mean that Thomas Walsh was innocent. He had lied three times, once about his marriage and twice about how he'd come by the scratches on his face.

As Novak drove north from SCI Greene, he wondered if he were acting with the same hubris that Harris had demonstrated years before. Had he assumed Walsh's innocence and closed his mind to the most likely explanation?

He carried these doubts with him as he entered his home Friday night. Kissing his mother on the forehead, he asked after his wife and learned that she had spent another afternoon searching through court records for him. *Probably caught in traffic on the Fort Pitt Bridge. Rush hour. What a misnomer.*

He removed three steaks from the refrigerator to bring them to room temperature, fired up the grill, and placed baking potatoes on the top rack. A quiet weekend lay ahead. Sunny weather, not too hot. A Riverhounds match against Charleston—one of their few home matches that month. Perhaps a hike through Ohiopyle State Park on Sunday. Still, as he sat on the rear deck, stretching his legs out before him, downing a can of sparkling water, he worried about the commitment he had made to Walsh—his time and that of his deputy and a patrol officer. Was this a misuse of borough resources? Was his motivation a search for justice or a desire to defy Mayor Tifton and show who was in charge?

At that moment, Barbara sailed into this sea of doubt, hailing him from inside. He struggled to his feet, pausing a moment to check his balance, and followed her voice into the dining room. He greeted her with a kiss and apologized for sending her out to play in traffic, but she cut him short.

Beaming, her face flushed, she lay notes and copies of documents out on the table. "You have to see this, Karol. You won't believe what I've found."

He looked over her shoulder, then stood alongside her, his arm around her waist, as she turned over one document after another, on each page pointing to a name she'd highlighted in yellow: Gerald Ten Eyck.

CALVIN MAYFIELD RETURNED to work Monday morning walking stiffly but bearing a grim smile. Fellow officers cheered when he entered, gripped his hand, and patted him on the back. "I've never worn a girdle before," he said. "This thing is killing me."

"It looks good on you," Novak said. "Barbara has a few spring frocks—"

Mayfield suppressed a laugh, wincing in pain. "Please don't do this to me."

Novak threw an arm around him and held him close.

"You didn't do that for me," Barnwell said.

David Kimrey, standing in the background, said, "And he'd better not."

Those around them laughed, and Novak realized he alone had not known about their relationship. *Some detective you are.*

To Mayfield, he said, "You're sure you feel up to this?"

"I wouldn't miss it."

He pulled them into his office and told them what Barbara had found at the courthouse. Gerald Ten Eyck, the jailhouse informant Harris had used in the Walsh case, popped up in one investigation after another. Along the way, the DA had cut deals with the informant.

"Harris framed people," Mayfield said.

"Looks like it. He decided who was guilty, falsified physical evidence, and, when that didn't work, used this professional snitch to seal the deal. But it's not enough."

Novak laid out a map of the 700 block of Spalding Street, on which he'd color-coded every house. "There are sixteen homes on this street," he said. "The seven marked in green are owned by the same families that lived there thirty years ago."

"Only in Pittsburgh," Lydia Barnwell said.

Novak had no response, since Pittsburgh was all he knew. He'd take her word for it.

"The five marked in yellow have been sold since the murder, but we have forwarding addresses. We'll take care of them later. Those in red have also turned over, but we haven't located the previous owners. That leaves this one," he said, pointing to an unmarked rectangle at 789 Spalding, "which was where the murder took place. We can skip that. The current owners wouldn't know anything about it."

The court had ordered the house sold months after Thomas Walsh's conviction, the proceeds going into a trust fund that had paid for Bridey's education and, later, the down payment on her current home. The house had changed hands twice since then.

"Let's start with the greens. Officer Barnwell will take these three," he said, stabbing at those on the north side of the street. "Mayfield and I will split these four between us." His assumption was that the injured deputy chief would fold after covering the first house and that he and Barnwell would each cover three.

"We're doing the interviews the county never conducted."

They traveled together in the chief's car, parking at the west end of the street and working their way downhill. Barnwell struck out at the first house. The owners no longer lived there but rented it to a young couple who were both at work.

Mayfield had no better luck. No one was home. He slipped his business card under the door with a request that the owners call.

Two doors down, a woman Novak judged to be in her late seventies answered, her hair like a Brillo pad whose strands had been pulled out. She stood at the door as he asked to speak but refused to let him in. "I need to clean up," she said. "Let's sit here on the porch."

He took a seat alongside her on the white wooden swing suspended from the overhanging ceiling on rusting metal chains. A chocolate Labrador retriever pushed its way through the screen door and curled up at his feet.

"Ralph's been gone for thirteen years. I live alone now."

Novak listened as she recounted her life story and the comings and goings of her children. Only her daughter still lived in the area, in Cranberry, north of Pittsburgh, and Novak got the feeling that her visits were few.

"Do you remember the Walsh family?" he said.

"Oh, yes. Who could forget? Her husband killed her, you know."

"We're looking into that. We have a few questions about his conviction. We're talking to neighbors to see what they recall about the family."

"You won't let him out, will you?" she said, her eyebrows arched in disbelief.

"I'm not saying that. We're just—"

"Because that would be a terrible thing."

"Mrs. Shooper, how well did you know them?"

"The Walshes? Oh, not at all. They had a little girl, didn't they? I would see her out playing. They let her have free rein, you know. It's a good thing this is a safe neighborhood, but these days, you never know."

She told Novak she didn't know Rebecca Walsh was having an affair and had no idea who her lover might have been. "We were all shocked at that," she said. "That's why he killed her. In a way, she had it coming, didn't she?"

"What do you remember about the weekend of the murder?"

"Nothing. Not a thing. It was Memorial Day, and Ralph and I had taken off for Deep Creek. We had a home there. The kids loved it. We spent every weekend at the lake during the summer." She shook her head and smiled, reliving the memory.

Novak thanked her and stood to go. The Lab rose and leaned against him as he stroked her head. As he stepped off the porch, the dog followed him until Mrs. Shooper called her back. She looked from one to the other and slowly returned.

He'd seen Mayfield pass by as they spoke, so he moved to the end of the street. Police work is a series of interviews and reports, interrupted occasionally by excitement no one wants. An hour later, the three regrouped and took off to the nearest Eat'n Park for lunch, requesting the party room for privacy.

After her first disappointment, Barnwell had had the most success. "Emily Mudry," she said, "knew the whole family well. Her husband was friends with Tom Walsh, and their daughter was just a few months older than Bridey, so they had lots of playdates. They knew their marriage was strained but also felt Tom was devoted to his wife. She was shocked when she learned Becky had had an affair; she knew nothing about it.

"She and her husband were here the morning the little girl discovered her mother's body. She was surprised Bridey didn't come to her first, but realized the O'Rourkes lived right across the street. They couldn't believe it when Tom was arrested. Her husband said he'd expressed nothing but love for Becky and was devoted to Bridey. But then their attitude changed. Slowly, she said, they came to accept the possibility of his guilt, and when Tom Walsh confessed, they decided that they'd been wrong about him."

"What do they think now?" Novak said.

"She's convinced he was guilty. There's no question in her mind."

"Interesting," Mayfield said. "I ran into the same thing." He related a conversation with a retired couple who told him Thomas Walsh had been a neighborhood leader. "He was an assistant coach on the Little League team. He took the kids to a Pirates game each summer, buying the tickets out of his own pocket. But he dropped out before the 1989 season."

"Which would correspond to his financial struggles," Novak said.

"When Becky was murdered, the whole neighborhood was on edge. Was a killer on the loose? Might one of them be next? When county police arrested Walsh, they couldn't believe it. 'Not Tom,' they'd said. But once word got out that he'd confessed, they decided he was guilty."

"And I suppose they dropped him," Barnwell said.

"They didn't volunteer it, but when I asked if they'd had any further contact with him, they acted as though I'd accused them of something. 'Of course not,' they said."

Over the next two days, they tracked down everyone who'd lived on the street the day of the murder. Three owners were no longer living. Four said they had not known the couple, apart from seeing Becky walk with her daughter or buying something at Tom Walsh's store.

Those who did know them added nothing new. As Novak summarized during a meeting late Wednesday afternoon, "Everyone in the neighborhood was terrified when Becky Walsh was murdered, but when Walsh confessed, they relaxed. Case closed. We're safe. They accepted it even before he went to trial, every good he'd done obliterated."

That left the O'Rourkes, to whom four-year-old Bridey had turned after finding her mother dead. "They moved to Washington in the months following the murder," Barnwell said, referring to a town thirty miles south of Boyleston. "I'm meeting with them this evening."

An hour later, after fighting the traffic south on I-79, Barnwell parked in front of a small bungalow on Fort Street. Grass grew like hay in the front yard. Paint peeled from the siding. She rang the doorbell, stood waiting for half a minute, rang again, and realized she couldn't hear any sound from inside the house. She knocked, and a heavy woman with flabby upper arms opened the door. She didn't smile, but stood aside when she saw the uniformed young woman.

Florence O'Rourke motioned the officer to an overstuffed chair that backed to the front window and asked if she wanted anything to drink.

"Water would be fine," she said.

While the woman bustled around in the kitchen, Barnwell cased the room. A stained rug that had once been light gray covered most of the hardwood floor, which had lost its shine at the edges. Rose-colored paint was chipped in places, scars peeking out from behind yellowing photographs of long-departed relatives. The foul odor of urine pervaded the room. Barnwell pictured the house collapsing around her. She couldn't wait to get this interview over with.

Mrs. O'Rourke handed her a large glass of ice water with a slice of lemon floating on top. She sat on a sagging sofa facing her, folding her hands in her lap and staring wordlessly at the officer. A tabby cat emerged and climbed on the back of the sofa, regarding Barnwell with a malevolent stare.

"Is your husband home?" she asked.

"Yes," she said, "but Terry...his memory isn't what it used to be." As she shifted her weight from one hip to the other, the couch trembled.

As though on cue, a man shuffled into the room. He was small, perhaps five-foot-eight, with a slender, almost ascetic frame. He wore baggy jeans and a Pirates T-shirt. Two days of beard covered his face, but not a hair sprouted on his wrinkled scalp. He looked from one to the other, then collapsed into a reclining chair alongside the fireplace.

"Terry, this is a police officer from Boyleston. She's come to talk to us about Tom Walsh."

"Walsh?" he said.

"He doesn't remember things."

A second cat of indeterminate parentage skulked into the room and sprang onto the back of Barnwell's chair in a single leap. The officer's eyes began to water, and she let out a loud sneeze, startling the animal. It arched its back and hissed at her.

"Molly is very gentle," Mrs. O'Rourke said.

"Thank you for agreeing to see me," Barnwell said after burying her nose in tissue. "We're talking to all those who lived on Spalding Street in May 1989."

"Is something wrong?"

Barnwell recited the message points she'd disgorged during her previous interviews. "When county detectives investigated the murder of Rebecca Walsh, they failed to interview neighbors. We're tying up loose ends."

"They interviewed us," she said, "me and Terry."

"Who did?" the man said. His wife ignored him. The tabby jumped from the sofa and wandered into another room.

"I've read the reports. You were most helpful. We—" Barnwell fumbled for a moment as she searched for a way forward. "We're trying to clear up some discrepancies in people's memories."

"I see." She shifted her weight again, and the sofa creaked. *Will it last the interview?*

"Tell me what you remember of that morning. The little girl came to your door…"

"She rang," Mrs. O'Rourke said. "I was making breakfast. Terry was upstairs somewhere. I called him to come down, but he didn't hear me."

"I heard you," he said. "She's a police officer."

The woman sighed, a half-smile on her lips as she cocked her head at Barnwell and shrugged. "She rang two or three times, so I went to the door. I remember I was making eggs, and they weren't done. I shoveled them onto a plate, figuring I'd scramble them later."

She inclined her head, as though recalling the day. "I was with Sears back then, working every weekend. We'd spent the night setting up for the Memorial Day sale, so I'd slept in a bit. I was still in slippers and a housecoat when she came to the door. I wasn't presentable. I saw Bridey through the glass in the front door. We had a wooden door with a diamond-shaped window in it, so you could see outside. They don't make those anymore."

Barnwell knew the style, but as she pictured it in her mind, thought the glass was placed too high to afford a view of a four-year-old. She kept the thought to herself.

"Anyway, Bridey was standing on her tiptoes, reaching for the doorbell, wearing nothing but a nightgown. It was a clear morning, so it was cold outside. The poor little thing was shivering, her arms wrapped around her, hopping from one foot to the other. I asked her what she was doing, and she started talking a mile a minute. I couldn't make out what she was saying, and I kept asking what was wrong. Then I caught a few words: Mommy, help, and sick."

She looked down at the coffee table, which held an assortment of knitting catalogs and magazines. "'Sick,' she'd said. Poor child. What she must have thought." She shook her head as she recalled the moment.

"Can you stay for dinner?" her husband said. "Flo is making chicken tonight."

"Hush, Terry. We're not having chicken."

"I love chicken."

Barnwell smiled at him and, lying, said, "I had dinner on the way down, thanks." Between sniffles, she thought to herself that she wouldn't have stayed if they'd offered pheasant under glass.

"What did you do when you sensed something was amiss?"

"I told the little girl to wait outside, then realized how cold she was and told her to come in. I don't think she'd ever been in the house before." Looking down, a faint smile on her face, the woman's voice softened as she seemed to recall the moment. "She didn't want to. Little thing took my hand and pulled me toward her house. Frantic, she was. I made her come in and called to Terry again. I couldn't cross the street dressed like that. My hair was still in curlers."

Of course, first things first. Let's worry about appearances.

And so it went for the next half hour, Flo meandering through her recollections of that fateful morning, Terry with no recollections at all, dropping irrelevancies into the conversation. And Barnwell fighting allergies.

In painstaking detail, Florence described how she'd forced her husband out the door. "He didn't want to go," she said. "He thought it would be improper."

But she'd convinced him. He was gone for five minutes, perhaps a few more, and came rushing back into the house, red-faced, out of breath, shouting at her to call the police.

"'What's wrong?' I said, but Terry just stood there looking down at the waif as she burst into tears. Because she knew then. She knew.

"I asked him again what was wrong. He just stood there, shaking his head, peering at me over the tops of his glasses. 'Just call the cops,' he said.

"I asked which ones, and he said he didn't care. Allegheny. Boyleston. He went into the bathroom and got sick to his stomach. We had your number on a sticker above the phone, so that's why I called Boyleston rather than 9-1-1. They asked me about that later. It was because the number was right there."

"That's all right," Barnwell said, marveling at how the smallest things could loom so large in the retelling. "We were closer."

"And all the time, poor little Bridey stood there looking at me. As though I could do something about it. Once Terry came out of the bathroom, she kept looking at him as though he could fix everything. You remember, don't you, honey? You burst into tears too."

Her husband looked at her and smiled, and then, suddenly comprehending, he began to sob. "Poor little Bridey," he said. "And Becky. Sweet Becky, who never hurt anyone."

His sobbing became uncontrollable, and Flo crossed to his side, bending over him, embracing him in a futile attempt to provide comfort.

"You'd better go," she said. "He gets like this sometimes. Believe me, whatever he remembers about that day, it's trapped up there."

Hardened as she was, it was all Barnwell could do to avoid breaking down herself as she drove north toward Boyleston.

CHAPTER TWELVE
INNOCENCE IS
INSUFFICIENT EVIDENCE

A t daybreak Thursday, Novak headed to Lawrence County, leaving the interstate on route 3 1 7 and turning north. It was a sunny morning. On KDKA, Ron Smiley predicted the temperature would reach the high seventies. Novak was glad to be out of the office again.

The highway bisected the lake north of Bessemer borough. He turned right after crossing the bridge onto a narrow, two-lane road and drove through the security gate at the Bessemer Lake Lodge parking lot.

The young woman at the reception desk gave him a broad, hospitality-issue smile and asked how she could help. Novak explained that he was looking for anyone who might have been employed by the lodge in 1989.

"I doubt there's anyone still here from that long ago," she said. "The family that owned the lodge sold it ten years back to Frontenac Resorts."

She entered an office behind the counter, emerging a minute later to say, "Tony says there's been a complete turnover since that time. Sorry."

Novak walked the property for a quarter hour, asking staff members if they knew anyone from that era. No one did. He'd wasted his time. The desk clerk validated his parking ticket, and he drove into town, pulling up at a diner. Ordering coffee and pancakes, he asked the server whether she knew anyone who had worked at the lodge in the eighties. She said she was new in town.

"Dan," a voice behind him said. Novak swiveled around to find two older men seated at a table by the window. "Dan Zaborowski," one said, eyeing Novak's uniform. "He worked out there for years."

"How do I find him?"

"What's this about?" He looked at Novak with suspicion, as though he'd realized he shouldn't be sharing information about locals.

Novak left his seat at the bar, pulled up a chair from an adjoining table, and introduced himself. "I'm looking into a murder that took place south of Pittsburgh thirty years back. The night of the killing, a man spent the night at the lake lodge, but no one can confirm it. That man was subsequently convicted. I'm trying to find anyone who worked there at the time."

Satisfied, the man reached for his vintage flip-phone, punched a few buttons, and said, "Danny, this is Jess. I'm down at Dawson's, and a cop is looking for you. I haven't told him about the still."

He laughed at his own joke, and Novak surmised that Danny had too. Novak reached for the cell phone and told the man at the other end what he was after. "Give me ten minutes," he said.

Novak thanked the pair and paid for their coffee. It took Zaborowski half an hour to arrive, by which time his companions had left. He appeared to be in his late seventies, but moved easily, favoring him with a wide, toothy grin. Novak led him to a table as far from the front door as possible and asked the server to turn down the loudspeaker, which was blaring an endless string of country songs.

Zaborowski told Novak to "call me Danny. Everyone else does," and recounted his history with the lodge. He'd begun working there part time in his teens, helping with maintenance jobs over the weekend. He'd continued after high school, becoming a night watchman and eventually the head of security until the lodge was sold.

"Bunch of Canuck bastards," he said. "They fired everyone and brought in their own people. Except for the maids and servers. They were all local. But over time, Frontenac replaced even them. Wiped the old crew off the map."

"What were your duties in May 1989?"

"I was still night watchman then. Midnight to six in the morning, seven days a week."

"A demanding shift," Novak said.

"No. I ran my own car repair shop in town. Worked six hours out at the lodge, eight at my shop, an early dinner, six hours of sleep. It was a great life. Made lots of money at a time when it was scarce."

"I'm going back to one particular night, the Friday of Memorial Day weekend in '89. I don't suppose you remember back that far."

"Sure can. That was during the recession. First time in years we had empty rooms on the holiday. I was looking forward to an easy night, maybe an hour of sleep. I was able to do that on occasion, but not this time. That was the night of the big blow-up."

"The big blow-up?"

"Yeah. There was a drunken party in the suite at the end of the top floor. Three guys and their girlfriends were playing music loud. They were out on the balcony yelling and screaming. Guests kept calling the desk. I had to go up twice to quiet them down. The third time, I told them my next call would be to the cops."

"Did you have to make that call?" Novak said.

"No, my threat did the job. They shut it down. Everything was quiet after that. The girls left. I called them girlfriends a moment ago, but that's not what they were."

"I get the picture."

"Once I let them out, everything quieted down."

Novak felt his heart race. "What do you mean, you let them out?"

"We'd had a lot of break-ins out in the lot, so in 1987, I think it was, we began locking the gate at midnight. Now they have it automated, but back then, it was my job to open it if someone entered or left during the night."

Zaborowski watched as Novak scribbled in his notebook. "Danny, this is important. How many times did you open the gate that night?"

"Just once, to let the—the women out."

"Was anyone with them? Did any other vehicle leave?"

"Just the girls."

Novak found three different ways to ask the same question, but the man was firm in his answers. Satisfied at last, he asked Zaborowski to accompany him to the borough police station to make a formal statement.

———

HE'D ASKED to meet with the district attorney. All he got, after using contacts from his days at Pittsburgh Police Bureau, was a late Friday meeting with a fresh-faced Assistant DA. It was better than nothing. He spent the day marshaling his evidence and, as he read it over, knew the answer she would give him before he asked it: *You don't have enough.*

"Let me summarize," he said, fearing he'd come so well prepared that he'd buried her in detail. "The first detective on the scene was pushed aside by a man we now know fabricated evidence in other cases. That detective focused on one suspect who, at the time, had no alibi. He failed to interview all the neighbors. From the start, the investigation was sloppy.

"The detective went north to collect the suspect's car and brought it back alone. He should have driven it directly to the crime lab, but he kept it overnight. Plenty of time to plant the tape and plastic bags in the trunk. The neighbor who discovered the body corrupted the crime scene. So the only physical evidence was tainted. This bent officer forced the suspect into a false confession."

"You can't be certain of that," she said.

"Read the transcript. You'll see. You could make the case on the interview process alone."

She wrote a few words on her legal pad but gave no signal she was convinced.

"The suspect later recanted his confession, but they had used it against him in court, and he lost his appeal. At the trial, your office called a witness, one Gerald Ten Eyck, who testified that Walsh confessed to him while he was being held for questioning."

Novak spread all the documents Barbara had assembled on the Assistant DA's desk. "This Ten Eyck character keeps coming up in other cases—another homicide and three drug convictions. All handled by the same detective. For years, Detective Matthew Harris used Ten Eyck, who posed as a sort of jailhouse lawyer. Whenever Harris had a shaky case, Ten Eyck would come forward claiming that the defendant had made a jailhouse confession while seeking his legal advice. He always told the same story, that they came asking for help and spilled their guts."

Here, Novak flipped through the transcript, pointing to the name Barbara had highlighted in yellow. "In each case, Ten Eyck, who was incarcerated for various other offenses, got a favor from your office—a reduced charge, a recommendation for a lower sentence, and in one case an outright release."

"We make deals with jailhouse informants all the time. I don't like it, but sometimes it's necessary."

"Each time, the same informant testified in a case brought by a detective who was later fired for falsifying evidence in drug cases." Novak was almost shouting now. "Doesn't that strike you as a bit too convenient?"

The Assistant DA maintained her impassive stare.

"I said Walsh had no alibi *at the time*. Now he does. A witness swears he never left the property." He related everything Dan Zaborowski had told him days before. "He couldn't have driven to Boyleston that night."

"One witness, recalling one night in one year three decades ago," she said. "And no corroborating evidence. No records from the hotel. No call to the police reporting a disturbance. It's one man's ancient memory."

Novak withheld comment, anticipating her next words. "You don't have enough."

———

FIGHTING his way through late afternoon traffic, he inched his way through the Fort Pitt tunnel and out I-376, parking in front of county police headquarters. They cleared him through to Detective Sergeant Glen Carpenter's office. "I got your message from dispatch," Novak said. "What's up?"

Carpenter pushed his chair back, stretched out his long legs, and locked his hands behind his head. "Remember back in April, the truck that overturned at the Greentree entrance to Parkway West?"

"I remember. Traffic backed up through Crafton, Boyleston, and Carnegie."

"That was our old friend, Aaron Ramos. We've pieced the entire story together."

Carpenter rolled forward in his office chair, turned over a couple of file folders, and found the one he was looking for. "Moretti hired Ramos in February. From the moment he came to work there, he was a screw-up. Left seeds in the watermelon, neglected to put strawberries into fruit trays, too much fruit in one, not enough in another. Norton Food Services complained and threatened to take its business elsewhere. Moretti traced the problems back to Ramos and fired him in late March."

Novak smiled, suspecting where this story was headed, but he didn't step on Carpenter's punchline.

"Ramos is angry with Moretti. They owe him past wages and maybe more. He's seen Norton trucks pulling up to Moretti's dock every morning. Drivers are friendly with the staff, so he thinks they're part of the same operation. After he's fired, he sees a Norton truck idling outside a convenience store one morning. He climbs in, puts it in gear, and drives off. Only, he doesn't know how to drive. He's spent all his adult life in a Honduran street gang and has never been behind the wheel. So he careens down Greentree Road, takes the entrance to the Parkway West too fast, hits the barrier, and flips the truck."

"Ah," Novak said. "That was the morning I moved into my office."

"He manages to climb out and makes a run for it," Carpenter said, "but not before taking an envelope clipped to the visor. He thinks there's cash inside—dumb bastard doesn't have the sense to know delivery vans don't collect the payments. But inside is the truck's delivery route—all the convenience stores on the schedule and their addresses."

Novak grinned and shook his head. "He started picking them off."

"He hit one, they had money, so he hit another. Everything was going well until Adi Patel made the mistake of trying to stop him. Ramos claims it was an accident, that he didn't mean to hurt him, but any way you cut it, it's a homicide in the commission of an armed robbery."

Novak flashed back to the images on the security cameras, Adi lunging across the counter to grab the man, rearing back after he was shot, smoke rising from the weapon.

"Ramos fled Honduras when another gang went gunning for him," Carpenter continued. "He made it to Mexico in the back of a truck, decided he wanted to come to the United States, so walked the rest of the way. He's likely to find a home here. Just not the one he wanted."

"And Mrs. Velazquez," Novak said. "What happens to her?"
"Who?"
"The Honduran holdup victim who put us onto him."
"I don't know who you mean," Carpenter said. "I've never heard of her. Know nothing about her. Neither does ICE."
"Thank you. Thanks very much."

"We're human beings." Carpenter leaned forward, playing with a paperclip as he spoke in a low voice. "We may be tough old cops, but we ain't heartless."

"THE EVIDENCE we've gathered isn't enough to free Walsh," Novak told Barnwell and Mayfield, "but even if we prove his innocence, it may not be enough."

"Why not?" Barnwell said.

"Even if we come up with irrefutable evidence of his innocence, he either has to win a new trial, which requires the district attorney's agreement, or the governor must commute his sentence. Walsh has been down that road twice and never passed Go. Either way, it could take years."

"What then?" Mayfield asked. "Do we give up?"

"No. We not only have to establish that he's innocent, but that *someone else is guilty*." Which, he admitted, was easier said than done.

"This wasn't a botched robbery; nothing was taken, and intruders don't strangle people in their beds. Becky Walsh had been depressed, but there's no evidence she was feuding with a neighbor. She had no known enemies. She was two months pregnant by someone other than her husband. Who is that person? Is he the killer?"

Novak spoke of him in the present tense, convinced that he was out there today, walking around free. Possibly someone they knew. The one other suspect Novak had considered—someone whose identity he had not yet shared with the others—had an alibi.

The trio reviewed every interview they'd conducted, looking for any hint as to the man's identity. In the past few days, they had extended their interviews, covering homeowners in the next block and those whose homes backed up to the Walsh residence across the alley. They'd added nothing to what they already knew. Barnwell and

Mayfield had spent two days interviewing members of the Presbyterian church the couple had attended. Again, nothing.

"It's not just the identity of Becky's lover," Barnwell said over the sandwiches Norma brought in from the deli. "There's something else we don't know."

The pair looked up, awaiting her revelation. "Chief, remember how this whole thing began. A little girl asked for your help."

"Amy O'Connor," Novak said.

"How did she learn about her grandfather being in prison? It wasn't from her mother. Someone had to have told her. Who?"

Which was the question that had nagged Novak from the outset.

———

ALTHOUGH BRIDEY O'CONNOR had rejected Mariel's efforts to question Amy, Novak told Lydia Barnwell to try. She didn't call ahead, appearing unannounced at her front door. Bridey stared at the woman in uniform without smiling. "What do you want?"

"I need to talk with you. May I come in?"

"What's this about?"

"Can we discuss it inside? It's hot as blazes out here, and what I have to tell you will take more than a few seconds."

"If you've come about my mother's murder, I have nothing to say."

"Mrs. O'Connor," Barnwell said in her most authoritative tone, "new facts have emerged. I must speak with you."

She stepped toward the door, and Bridey moved out of her way. "Is your daughter here?"

"No," Bridey said, retreating into the living room as Barnwell advanced. "She's at a friend's house."

"Good." Barnwell already knew this, as the friend was Novak's granddaughter. She took a seat on the sofa and waited for Bridey to settle.

"What new information?" Crossing her arms, she scowled at the officer, but eased herself into an armchair.

"We have sworn testimony that your father never left Bessemer Lake the night your mother was killed."

"That's impossible. I know he murdered her."

"Why are you so certain?"

"Because I saw them fight before he left. And he came into my room that night."

Barnwell forced herself to show no emotion. "Tell me what happened."

"It was hot when Mother put me to bed. At least I think it was, because I'd asked her for my pink blanket. I always slept with Pinkie, as I called it, but she said I didn't need it that night. We fought over it. It's strange, the things you remember." She stared off into the distance.

"It must have gotten cold during the night, because when I woke up, Pinkie was wrapped around me. I remember someone kissing me good night as he laid the blanket over me."

"And you're certain it was your father?"

"Who else would it have been? Who else knew how attached I was to that pink blanket?"

Who, indeed? "Mrs. O'Connor—"

"Bridey."

"Are you sure it was your father you saw that night? Could it have been someone else?"

Her look of certainty turned to one of confusion. "Look, do you want coffee or something?"

"Tea would be great." Bridey retreated to the kitchen, while Barnwell let her think about it. The sound of a whistling tea kettle. A drawer opening and closing. Otherwise, silence from the kitchen. Then she reappeared, a mug of tea in one hand and a cup of coffee in the other. She placed both on the table between them.

"No," she said.

"No?"

"I'm not certain the man I saw was my father. I never saw his face. He didn't speak." She sipped at her coffee.

"I'm having trouble separating my real memories from what I've been told. My grandmother—my mother's mother, who raised me—she always talked about my dad. He did this. He did that. She never let up. When I'd do something bad, she'd say, 'You don't want to grow up to be like your father.'"

She fell silent. Barnwell waited as her tea grew cold.

"This witness of yours—is she certain he never left the lodge?"

"It's a he," Barnwell said, "and yes. He has good reason to remember what happened that night. What he recalls tallies with other things we know."

Bridey sighed, encircling the rim of her coffee mug with her finger. "I'm not saying it wasn't my father. I'm just not certain it was."

"Understood," Barnwell said. "We run into this all the time. Memory is fragile and grows less reliable with age. You're not alone."

Bridey O'Connor smiled through welling tears. "It was not a happy home. I was little but old enough to feel the tension."

Barnwell left her with her memories for a moment, then saw an opening as the woman shook her head. "Bridey, we must speak with Amy. We need to know how she learned about her grandfather. Who told her...and why? It may mean nothing, but it could be vital."

She began nodding even before Barnwell finished speaking. "Yes. Yes," she said. "I need to know that, too."

August 14, 2018, a Tuesday. A statewide grand jury had been meeting for two years. Its report had been the subject of a pitched court battle for weeks, as those whose illegality it revealed sought to suppress it. Two weeks before, the Pennsylvania Supreme Court had ordered the release of a redacted version. Now, at last, it was public.

Novak didn't go to work on this day. He and Barnwell weren't scheduled to meet with Amy O'Connor until the following morning.

While many other matters filled his inbox, there was, on this day, nothing more important to him. He sat at his dining room table, his eyes focused on the screen of his laptop, as he read through the report.

> We, the members of this grand jury, need you to hear this. We know some of you have heard some of it before. There have been other reports about child sex abuse within the Catholic Church. But never on this scale. For many of us, those earlier stories happened some place else, some place away. Now we know the truth: it happened everywhere...
>
> We heard the testimony of dozens of witnesses concerning clergy sex abuse. We subpoenaed, and reviewed, half a million pages of internal diocesan documents.
>
> They contained credible allegations against over three hundred predator priests. Over one thousand child victims were identifiable, from the church's own records. We believe that the real number—of children whose records were lost, or of those who were afraid ever to come forward—is in the thousands.

Redactions left words, sentences, paragraphs, even entire pages blank, but enough priests and parishes were named in the hundreds of pages to paint a damning picture. And there, in the Diocese of Pittsburgh, a report on the acts of molestation committed by Father Timothy Dacey during his seven years at St. Cyril and Methodius Church.

Father Tim, the report said, had groomed over a dozen young boys during overnight camping trips. Many had grown up with mental and emotional problems. Some had turned to drugs. One had taken his own life.

Missing from the report was that one had become a police officer, a detective, chief of detectives, and later chief of a small police force near Pittsburgh. A man who now trembled, tears overflowing his eyes, spilling down his cheek, and dripping onto his shirt as he grieved over the loss of his best childhood friend, Henry Sutton, who had committed suicide at eighteen, his entire life behind him.

"I could have helped him," Novak said between sobs. "I *should* have helped him."

"You couldn't," Barbara said as she stood behind him, rubbing his shoulders. "You couldn't even help yourself."

CHAPTER THIRTEEN
A CASE OF SELF-CENSORSHIP

Novak and Barnwell arrived at nine o'clock. Bridey's expression as she answered the door reflected her anxiety, her eyes darting from one of them to the other and back again. "Are you sure I shouldn't stay in the room?"

"Mrs. O'Connor, it's your right to listen in," Novak said. "Amy has done nothing wrong. This isn't an interrogation. But we need her to be open with us. If you think she'll do that while you sit across from her, you're free to do so. If not, please let us speak with her alone."

She considered that for a moment. "You're Jen's pap. It's not like you're strangers. But if she becomes frightened—"

"I'll come and get you myself," Barnwell said. Novak wasn't certain how the two women had established a rapport, but he was grateful for it.

Bridey placed a plate of cookies and a pitcher of lemonade on the dining table. She called for Amy to come downstairs, hovered a moment to make certain her daughter was comfortable, and closed the swinging door as she left.

She was a slender, freckle-faced girl with reddish hair that descended in ringlets, as Irish as her name. "Hi, Amy," Barnwell said. "My name is Lydia."

The child looked at her and smiled. "I'm Amy."

"And I'm Karol," he said, "Jen's grandpa."

She nodded and smiled shyly. "Why do you have a girl's name?"

Novak's face crinkled in a grin. "In the part of the world my mother came from, it's a man's name, too. But kids used to tease me about it when I was your age. Does anyone ever tease you?"

She grew serious and nodded her head. Novak sensed he'd touched a nerve and elected to back off and ease into the conversation.

"At your birthday party months ago, you asked for my help. Do you remember?"

She nodded so vigorously she looked like a bobblehead. "Uh-huh."

"What is it you wanted me to do?"

She looked about uncertainly. "It's all right," Barnwell said. "Your mother said it was okay to talk with you. She understands it's important. Would you feel more comfortable if she were here?"

"No," she said, blurting out the word. Looking around again, she lowered her voice and said, "I wanted to see if you could get my pap out of jail."

"How did you learn he was in prison?" Novak asked. "Did your mother tell you?"

"No," she said, then looked at them as they waited. "Pauly did."

"And who is Pauly?"

"A boy at school. His real name is Paul, but we call him Pauly."

"What did Pauly say about your grandfather?"

"He's the one who teases me. He said my grandpa was a jailbird. He kept saying that, and I said he wasn't, that he was dead. That's what Mom told me. But he kept saying it. I told him if he didn't stop, I'd tell Mrs. Murdock. She's our teacher. She doesn't like bullying."

"Neither do I," Novak said.

"When you told him to stop, did he do so?" Barnwell said.

"At first. But then he started calling him a patsy."

The officers caught each other's eyes. "What did you think he meant by that?" Barnwell said.

"I know what it means," she said with defiance. "It's someone who lets others take advantage of them."

"Why do you think Pauly called your grandpa that name?" she said.

"He told me. He said he was in jail for something another person had done and that he was too dumb to defend himself."

"Did he tell you how he knows this?" Barnwell said.

"No, he just kept saying that he's a patsy and he's stupid."

"What did you do when he said that?" she asked.

"I hit him. I punched him with my fist and made him cry."

Barnwell laughed. Regaining control after a few seconds, she told the perplexed child, "Good for you. Don't ever let boys push you around."

───────

COME WHEN U CAN. *Mother v upset.* Novak had studied the text message and made his apologies to Barnwell. "Something's come up at home. I'll see you at the cop shop in an hour or so."

"Where's Mother?" he said as he burst through the front door. "What's wrong?"

"She's in her room. She got up late and read the morning paper."

His confusion lasted only a millisecond. He'd been so consumed with grief yesterday, he hadn't considered what the grand jury report would do to his mother. He bounded up the stairs and knocked at her door.

"*Mamička*, what's wrong?"

"Have you heard what they're saying about Father Tim?" She lay in her bed fully clothed, a box of tissues alongside her.

He sat on the love seat in front of the window. "Yes. I read the report yesterday."

"They say he did terrible things to boys on those camping trips. That can't be true."

"I'm afraid it is," he said.

Her eyes widened. "You knew about this?"

His eyes downcast, he said, "Yes, I did."

"How long, Karol? How long have you known?"

All my life. "A long time."

"Did you tell anyone about it?"

"I'm one of those who testified. I talked to the grand jury last November."

"But before that?"

"Many years ago, I told Father Michal."

"And what did he say?"

Novak closed his eyes, recalling his meeting with the venerable Slovakian priest after confession.

"Are you certain you're not imagining this, my son? You must be mistaken. No? Have you spoken to others about this? Fine. There's a good boy. You must keep this between the two of us. God wants you to keep this close to your heart. It must be our secret."

"That's why he left St. Cyril's. Father Michal told someone in the archdiocese. Maybe the bishop. Perhaps someone else. I don't know who. And they moved Father Tim. But do you know what they did?"

Novak didn't wait for her response, his face hardening, his voice brittle with the bitterness of five decades of lies and deceptions. "They moved him to another parish. They transferred him to St. Ignatius out in Monroeville, where he did the same thing to other boys. And then they moved him again. That's what they did, *Matka.* Instead of reporting this pedophile, they covered it up. Instead of protecting young boys, they *just gave him new ones.* Innocent youngsters, not even men yet. Boys who didn't know these things were wrong. They let him ruin their lives."

"Oh!" She recoiled as though he'd struck her. She sobbed until there were no tears left. Novak lay down next to her and held her in his arms.

When she'd exhausted herself, she looked up at him, small and frail, seeming to melt away like an ice carving in summer.

"Karol, you went camping with him. You and Henry. Did he—?"

"Yes, he did."

"Oh, no!" He felt her body heave, but no tears came. "Why didn't you tell me?" she said in a small, pleading tone.

"I told Dad. Father Michal made me promise not to tell anyone. But I told Dad."

"What did he say?"

How much should I tell her? "He didn't believe me. I don't blame him. I was young. No one knew about such matters. An eight-year-old boy saying things like this about a priest?

"One thing I've learned in these past few days," he said, "is to trust what children tell you."

Through Mariel, Novak learned that Pauly was Paul Cramer, a nine-year-old boy who, like Amy and Jen, was about to enter fourth grade. "Good luck talking to his parents," she'd said. "They're the type whose children can do no wrong. If a teacher calls them to discuss a behavioral problem, their first response is to ask what that nasty teacher is doing to their precious little boy."

Her warning was prescient. Pauly's father, Paul Sr., responded to Novak's call by saying, "What do you want with him? He hasn't done anything."

"I'm not suggesting he has," Novak said. "We need to question him about information he may have about a case we're investigating."

"What case is that?"

"I'd like to discuss that with him. You're welcome to sit in on our conversation. In fact, I hope you will."

"Not until you tell me what this is about," Cramer said.

"He suggested to a classmate that he knew about a legal situation involving her grandfather. He seems to have learned something that could be significant."

"What legal situation?"

"Look, Mr. Cramer. I need to speak to your son about this. I have at most three questions to ask. It should take less than ten minutes. When can I meet with him?"

"Paul Jr. knows nothing about any legal case. Do you have a warrant?"

"A subpoena, you mean? No, and it's unnecessary because we don't suspect your son of anything."

"If you want to talk to him, you'll need a subpoena. And if you do so, my attorney will talk to you."

With that, the line went dead.

"Curious," Novak said to Barnwell. "I didn't tell him what this is all about, but I'm convinced he knows. How do we get at this?"

She was back in fifteen minutes with the answer. "Paul Cramer and his wife, Mary Katherine, married on May 4, 2007, at Church of the Redeemer in Washington County. I'll give you three guesses as to Mary Katherine Cramer's maiden name."

Novak needed only one.

———

THEY MADE the trip south in less than an hour, plotting strategy as they drove. Barnwell was annoyed with herself. "They're good. They almost had me in tears."

Novak told her to forget it. She wasn't the only one who had missed the clues. "Let them do their performance art for a bit, then we'll bring down the curtain."

She had him stop at a drugstore for antihistamines, and they drove on to the house. Barnwell didn't bother with the doorbell. She knocked, waited ten seconds, and knocked again.

Florence O'Rourke didn't conceal her astonishment. "Officer

Barnwell, so nice to see you." Her rapid blinking suggested it was anything but.

Lydia introduced Novak, "*Chief* Novak," she emphasized, and asked if they could come in.

"Well, I'm rather busy. I was just cleaning up."

You couldn't clean this place if you worked at it for a month.

"This will just take a few minutes. Thank you for agreeing to see us." And walked in before the woman could protest. "Perhaps if we meet in the dining room." *Anything to keep the damned cats away.*

No luck. As she and Novak sat alongside each other, a black cat that hadn't appeared on her previous visit jumped onto the dining room table and curled up. Mrs. O'Rourke lowered herself into a chair opposite them. It groaned with the effort.

"Is Mr. O'Rourke at home?" Novak asked.

"No," she said, fluttering her hands to indicate some point in the distance. "Terry's out right now." He stared at her until she averted her eyes, her fingers twisting about each other as she studied them.

"When the county detectives questioned your husband the day of the murder, he told them Thomas Walsh had gone up to Bessemer Lake with friends," Novak said. "How did he know that?"

"I don't know. You'd have to ask him."

"But we can't do that, can we?"

She tried to meet his gaze, but her eyes danced about the room. "No, his memory's not—I think Tom must have told him."

"Tom Walsh? When did he do that?"

"I don't recall."

"Why would Walsh have told your husband not just what he was doing and where he was going, but who would accompany him?"

She began to speak but stopped.

"It seems like a lot of detail, doesn't it? He gave the detectives such precise information that Lawrence County deputies were able to find him right away."

"I'm afraid I just don't know."

"Let's go back to the previous evening." The cat stretched, rose, and planted itself in front of Barnwell with its back to her. She wiped tears from her eyes, dabbed at her nose, and wheezed as she spoke. "You told us you were working late at Sears."

"That's right. We were restocking for Memorial Day."

Novak removed the cat, who yowled and dashed away.

"What was your husband doing?" Barnwell said.

"I don't recall. It was so long ago. You can't expect me to remember things that far back."

"Did he have a night job, too?"

"Oh, no, he was a pharmacist. He never worked past six."

"So your husband was home alone that Friday night?" she said.

"I suppose." She gulped and looked from one to the other. "Why does it matter?"

"You and your husband spent your lives in Boyleston, didn't you? He was born in the house on Spalding." She nodded, looking confused by the shift in direction.

"All your lives," Novak said. "Yet three months after the Walsh murder, you sold your house and moved, not just out of the neighborhood, but all the way down here to Washington County. You both left your jobs. Why?"

"We enjoy country life." A car stopped outside. A door slammed. Mrs. O'Rourke turned, craning her neck to see out the front window. Novak watched her fidget and maintained his silence until a screen door banged across the street.

"Do you know Paul Cramer?"

"Paul? That's our son-in-law. What has he—?"

"Paul Jr.," Barnwell said. "Pauly."

"He hates it when people call him that."

"Pauly," Barnwell repeated. "Why would your grandson have spoken to another child about the Walsh murder?"

The woman ran her right hand across her forehead, the flab below her forearm wobbling as though reflecting her nervousness. "Little Paul doesn't know—" She stopped herself, her face a mask of uncertainty. "What did he say?"

"What doesn't he know?" Novak said.

"He knows nothing about that night."

"He knows quite a lot. He knows Thomas Walsh is in jail. He says he's there for a crime he didn't commit. He's called Walsh a patsy, said it more than once."

She forced a smile. "You know how little boys are. They'll say anything to get attention. It's just talk."

"This wasn't a one-time thing," Barnwell said. "He's been taunting Thomas Walsh's granddaughter. He insists that Walsh is innocent."

"Well," she said dismissively. "Is that all?"

"Here's what happened," Novak said. "Your husband knew Walsh would be gone for the weekend. He knew because Becky Walsh had told him. Not Tom, *Becky*. She told him because she also knew you'd be working that night, setting up for the weekend sale. Why would they share such intimate knowledge with each other?"

She was red in the face, her head bowed, her fingers knitting an imaginary blanket.

Novak lowered his voice and leaned toward her. "Because they were getting together, as they had off and on for weeks, for months. Your husband crossed the street after the neighborhood was quiet. He entered the Walsh house. Becky was expecting him. They'd met like this on many evenings. But on this night, she told him she was pregnant. Or had she already told him? Either way, he went to the downstairs closet off the dining room and came back with a plastic bag and a roll of industrial tape. He tied her hands behind her, pulled the bag over her head, and watched—"

"No. Is that what Little Paul told you?"

"Where is Terry? We need to speak to him. I don't know what the DA will make of this, a man in his condition. It's not for me to say. Where is he, Flo?"

"That's not how it happened."

Neither said a word. Silence hung between them like a shroud. Then Barnwell sneezed. They waited for her to finish, both god-blessing her. She wiped her nose, cleared her throat, and let the tears well in her eyes.

Once more, the room became quiet. The officers waited, the silence as oppressive as the smell of cat pee.

"I did it."

Flo enclosed the fingers of both hands in her fists as the two officers tried to hide their astonishment. Barnwell flashed back to Terry's emotional reaction during her previous visit when he spoke the words, "Sweet Becky, who never hurt anyone."

"We wrapped up about one o'clock, so I came home," Mrs. O'Rourke said. "I made certain Terry was asleep, then crossed the street. I got the bag and tape out of the closet. I knew where it was. I'd been over there many times. She was my friend. *My friend.*"

She sobbed. Novak couldn't tell whether they were real or stage tears. It made no difference.

"She was asleep. I was a strong woman. That's how I got the job handling merchandise. I threw her on her back and taped her hands and feet before she knew what had happened. I flipped her back over to make her look at me. I told her, 'This is what happens when you mess with Flo O'Rourke.'

"I put the bag over her head and wrapped tape around it. And wrapped and wrapped. She struggled, but there was nothing she could do to stop me. I stood and watched until it was over." She shrugged as though it didn't matter.

AN HOUR LATER, with Washington County detectives having joined them, she told the rest of the story. Terry had come home in a panic earlier in the week and confessed. Becky had just informed him she was pregnant. What was he to do? He'd broken down, apologized to his wife, and assured her he loved her. She'd promised she would think of something.

What she'd thought of was devious. Becky, her "friend," would be dead, and when the police discovered she was pregnant, Terrence, whose fingerprints were all over her bedroom, would be blamed for her death. She would rid herself of both those who had betrayed her.

She'd arranged Becky's nightclothes to suggest Terry had killed her after having sex. She looked in on Bridey before she left the house, saw that she was cold, and laid the pink blanket over her. And when the little girl showed up at her door hours later, frightened and shivering, she added a twist, insisting that her husband cross the street where he would find the body. When he saw his lover lying dead in her bed, he tore at the plastic bag, trying to save her. He pulled her panties up and covered her with a sheet, leaving evidence on everything he touched. Her plan was working better than she'd hoped.

But then something happened she hadn't foreseen. Rather than spending the night with friends, Thomas Walsh had booked a separate room at the lodge. He had no alibi. A bent cop had framed him. Flo couldn't have redirected the investigation without implicating herself, so she'd allowed events to take their course.

As her scheme unraveled, she'd found she couldn't continue to live in that house. What if neighbors remembered seeing Terry crossing the street to the Walsh house at odd hours? What if someone found evidence exonerating Walsh?

Terry couldn't work. He'd spend hours staring out the window at the house across the street, mourning his lover. They'd had to leave. She'd nagged her husband until he agreed to sell the house and move miles away from Boyleston.

A decade ago, when Walsh had appealed for clemency, the newspapers had dredged up the sordid details of the murder. And one morning, as Terry was seated at the table where they now sat, he'd looked at her and said, "Tom didn't do this."

"What makes you so sure?" she'd asked.

"They say he killed her because she was pregnant by another man, but he didn't know that. She hadn't told him, so he had no motive. And he wouldn't have left himself without an alibi if he'd intended to kill her. It makes no sense."

And the more she'd argued with him, insisting on Walsh's guilt, the more he had begun to suspect the truth. Until, as dementia overcame him, emerging in angry bursts, he'd blurted to his grandson one afternoon that Grandma had killed a neighbor lady and her husband had gone to prison for the crime.

Florence O'Rourke was held at the Washington County jail until Novak could arrange her transfer to Allegheny County.

As Novak and Barnwell drove north that evening, the chief said, "Nice work, *Detective*."

She smiled and let out a self-satisfied sigh as his words registered.

CHAPTER FOURTEEN
I'VE DONE MY DUTY

"You asked for this meeting," Mayor Tifton said.

"Yes," Novak said. "I'm wrapping up the Walsh murder investigation."

"Lentz gave me a rundown this morning. That's a nice piece of work."

"Thank you. I had the help of two outstanding officers. We're not quite finished."

"I'm sure. Lots of paperwork, helping the DA build his case against the O'Rourke woman."

"And we need to secure Tom Walsh's release," Novak said. "That's not automatic. The DA has to recommend his release to the governor, who must agree. It will take time. Meanwhile, Tom Walsh remains in jail for a crime he didn't commit."

"That's tragic. A total miscarriage of justice. So unfair," Tifton said. "And I wish... It's just another black mark on Boyleston. All this publicity, reporters going door-to-door, news crews in front of the municipal building, live reports on every newscast. It's not good for our image."

"Appearances are everything, aren't they?"

"Not everything, but they're important. Don't you agree?"

Novak leaned back, thrusting his legs out before him as though he were changing the subject. "One thing that has most impressed me about this—and not in a good way—is the sense of abandonment Walsh felt as soon as he was charged. Everyone deserted him. He'd lost his wife and child, his business, and all his friends. That's one reason he confessed, the fact that he was isolated. Nothing mattered to him anymore."

Novak let that sink in for a moment.

"His best friends were the three men he went fishing with each Memorial Day. They'd gone together to Bessemer Lake for years and had known each other since grade school. Lifelong friends. But not one of them came to visit. Not one has spoken to him since that day. Years of friendship—" Novak snapped his fingers. "—gone like that."

Tifton looked warily at the chief.

"Do you know why they kept silent?" Novak said. "They brought three prostitutes into their suite that night. All three men were married. Think of how that would have looked."

"You've made your point," Tifton said.

"And one was so dishonest that he worked behind my back to keep me from reopening the investigation. He was willing to let a life-long friend rot in jail—all to keep up *appearances*." He spat the word out.

Novak stood up. "I could never work for a man like that. I have no respect for anyone who could do such a thing—just to protect his image."

Novak ARRIVED at the diner early, ordered a cup of coffee, and waited. Bernie Jackson arrived on time, taking the seat opposite his in the booth. "Thanks for meeting with me on a Saturday," he said.

"Any time, Bernie."

"You're missing a soccer match."

Novak waved it away. "Arsenal plays tomorrow. We're fine."

Jackson ordered a Reuben and a root beer. They made small talk while they waited, discussing the weather—too hot and humid—and the summer—too brief and busy. When his food arrived, Bernie took a huge bite and seemed to swallow it without chewing.

"You're sure you don't want anything?"

"No, thanks. I'm having pizza in an hour. Your dime," he said.

"Mmph." He absorbed another mouthful. "You know why I asked to meet with you."

"I have a pretty good idea."

"We want you to stay. That's official. The council wants you to rescind your resignation."

Raising his cup, Novak signaled to the server for a refill. "Barbara and I have discussed this. We agree it's best."

"Is it something I said?"

"I'm not suited for this. I can't deal with the politics. I don't like it when people aren't upfront with me. Apart from your eminence," he said with a nod toward his friend, "I haven't felt support from a single council member since I started. I made a modest remodeling request —a few cans of paint and removing mold from the bathrooms. The budget committee still hasn't budged, so Barbara and I did it ourselves."

Except for the last two walls. Novak had arrived the Monday following Florence O'Rourke's arrest to find that the officers had finished the job he and Barbara had begun.

"I've constantly been put on the defensive when all I've tried to do is my job."

Bernie sighed and finished his sandwich in another bite. "If Frain were capable of apologizing to anyone, he would do so to you. He doesn't have it in him and never will. But he's the one who began making calls, insisting we had to get you to change your mind. Tifton has resigned, you won't have to deal with him."

The council didn't know the half of that man's deceit—how, when Lydia Barnwell came to him to report what she'd learned about Chief Russell's theft from the borough, the mayor had betrayed her confidence—even telling McMahon, when the county began to investigate the chief, that she had been the source.

"You've done a great job for us. Four months ago, this department couldn't catch a cold without screwing it up. Look what you've done with them."

"You said it yourself, Bernie, we have some great officers. They'll do fine without me."

"You're wrong," he said, leaning over the table. "You've removed the deadwood. Except for Ewer, maybe."

"Ewer's fine. I just ignore him."

"You got rid of McMahon. You restored public confidence. You promoted Calvin Mayfield and Lydia Barnwell. Think about them. You've put them where they deserve to be, in positions of authority. Now you're about to abandon them to a new chief who may not..." Jackson let out a deep sigh. "Let's face it. We don't pay enough to get someone of your caliber. So we'll get someone with half your talent and leadership skill. Will you do that to Barnwell and Mayfield?"

"Bernie, I came here to do a job. I've done it. I've done my duty."

He considered what he'd just said. "I've brought justice. I never thought I'd say that, but I have. But I'm tired and discouraged." He looked his friend in the eye. "There's something else going on in my life, something I can't discuss."

"Health?"

"No. What was I saying about justice? I need to seek justice for a late friend, and it's not something I can do from this position."

"Boyleston needs you. Will you at least think about it?"

Novak spun his now-empty coffee cup and waved off the server. "All right. I will. But I can't promise anything."

"Fair enough," Jackson said.

"Right now, I have something more important to do. A nine-year-old girl's birthday party was interrupted a few months ago. Barbara is making it up to her today, and I wouldn't miss it."

ACKNOWLEDGMENTS

If you enjoyed this book, please leave a review at your e-store or on Goodreads. Reviews are the primary means by which independent authors alert other readers to our books. To follow future investigations of Karol and Barbara Novak, Calvin Mayfield, and Lydia Barnwell, go to my author's website, lewisthescrivener.com where you may subscribe to my mailing list. Thank you.

This is a work of fiction. All the characters are creatures of my imagination, as is the borough of Boyleston.

I wish to thank Albina Senko, my neighbor, for allowing me to borrow and adapt parts of her story for the character of Izabela Novak. This lovely lady's life is far more interesting than Izabela's and deserves a book of its own. Perhaps someday...

I am also indebted to Inspector Andrew Schurman of the Allegheny County Police Department, who provided background information on the relationship between his department and the myriad law enforcement agencies within the county. Inspector

Schurman told me I could staff the Boyleston PD in almost any configuration I chose and I wouldn't be far wrong.

Numerous patrol officers in Pittsburgh, Mount Lebanon, Dormont, and Crafton provided insights from their real-life experiences.

In the end, however, this is a novel, so any inaccuracies are either unintentional or committed in service to the story.

Thanks to my line editor, Kylee Madison of NoteworthyRevisions.com, for another first-class job. Kylee also edited my previous novel, *Breaking News*.

The narrator of the audio version, Robert McBride, made invaluable additional recommendations.

Writing coach Ashley Kunsa made extensive comments about restructuring the first chapter as part of Chuck Sabuchino's 2020 Pittsburgh Writing Workshop and helped confirm that Karol and Barbara make quite a pair.

The stunning cover design is the work of Laura Boyle of LauraBoyleDesign.com, using a background image of mine taken in Weirton, WV. I recommend Laura to anyone seeking quality design work.

Finally, thanks to my wonderful wife, Julie, for her help and patience, to my daughters, Kristen Dunder and Lisa Kalnai, and to Caeden and Emma Kalnai, my two greatest fans.

ABOUT THE AUTHOR

James H (Jim) Lewis is a former reporter, public media executive, and consultant to non-profit organizations who serves as a copywriter for nonprofit clients. This is his third novel.

He has lived and worked in Washington, DC, Florida, Texas, New England, Oregon, and Sweden, where he reported for the daily Eurovision news exchange. His articles have appeared in the *Washington Post, Fundraising Management,* and *Current,* and his news reports and documentaries have been aired by public television stations and ABC News. He completed a self-designed BA at the University of Massachusetts in 1991. Jim and his wife, Julie, currently reside in Pittsburgh.

CPSIA information can be obtained
at www.ICGtesting.com
Printed in the USA
LVHW091048210820
663812LV00002B/426